FORBIDDEN RIVER

Running a boat from St. Louis to Fort Benton, Montana, was a hazardous task at the best of times, but in the years toward the end of the War between the States, it was fraught with even graver perils. Kathleen Garrison knew what she was doing when she asked Captain Denny Rawls to pilot her boat, the *Varina*, loaded with supplies for her brother in the new gold fields of Montana, for Denny was considered the best captain in the area.

But pretty Astrid McQuestion, to whom Denny had just become engaged, came first with him and her father wanted him to take the McQuestion boat, the *Astrid*, to Fort Benton. Denny knew nothing of McQuestion's plan to discredit him and at the same time get rifles to the Indians, thus diverting the Union forces from their war against the Confederacy. Nor did he know that both the *Astrid* and the *Varina* would leave the Missouri for the even more treacherous Yellowstone. For the Yellowstone ran through Indian land so hostile to the white man that it was strictly taboo.

FORBIDDEN RIVER

Al Cody

WESTERNS

First published 1952
by Bouregy and Curl, Inc.

This hardback edition 1993
by Chivers Press
by arrangement with
Donald MacCampbell Inc.

ISBN 0 7451 4569 8

British Library Cataloguing in Publication Data available

Printed and bound in Great Britain by
Redwood Press Limited, Melksham, Wiltshire

FORBIDDEN RIVER

Chapter One

Untimely darkness poised like a hovering bird over the land, squeezing out its woe in long wet sheets of rain. As a consequence, the streets of St. Louis were all but deserted, save for those unlucky mortals compelled by necessity to be abroad at this hour. A team of nondescript nags splashed through the mud, the carriage which they pulled drawing up discreetly short of the light reflected from the windows of the Planters House, that well-known and justly popular hostelry at Chestnut and Fourth.

Three men alighted, dismissing the cab. The first was short and broad, giving the appearance of a pouter pigeon; the next man was half a head taller, his long horse face showing sad and mournful. The last to descend was wrapped in a long military cloak, and he topped them both. The light showed a close-trimmed mustache palely red, a sharp hawk nose, and yellowish-brown eyes.

After a quick, suspicious glance around, his voice came clipped and short:

"Do you boys understand what you are to do? When he shows up at The Planters, contrive to make a fool of him—but at the proper time, understand, after my party arrives and when I give you the signal! Make him look like a fool, a bungling idiot. Do a good job and I'll pay you ten dollars apiece. If you put on a really good performance, I'll double it."

"Trust us for that, Cap'n Whirter." The voice was unexpectedly thin and reedy, coming as it did from the beefy man with the pock-marked face. "You can always depend on old Sol Sherwood for any job, specially if it's a show. I'd of been on the stage yet if it wan't for this face o' mine. And Taber here is nigh as good as me. Fact is, for that money, we'll do more'n just make a show of him, if that's what you want."

"I don't, you fools!" Whirter retorted impatiently. "Do what I tell you, and I'll be satisfied. But if you bungle it, I'll halve your pay."

"But how will we know him?" Taber demanded, speaking from under a shapeless hat that dripped its collected puddles inside his pulled-up coat collar. "We don't want to make no mistake—"

"I've told you already. He's tall—as tall as I

am—and smooth-shaven, except for sideburns. His hair is black as soot, and he'll be in the uniform of a river captain. But it's mostly the look of him—kind of a high and mighty air—" Abruptly he broke off to point, lowering his voice to a hissing whisper. "There he is now! Just getting out of that carriage!"

This second equipage had pulled up squarely in front of the light thrown from the windows. Captain Denny Rawls, disdainful of the beating rain, paused to pay his fare, and with a smile and a gratuity for the driver which brought an answering grin of appreciation to the broad black face, he stepped briskly across the sidewalk, boot thuds muffled by the soggy wetness of the boards, and disappeared within.

Once inside, Rawls loitered near the main entrance, surveying the big, brilliantly lighted room and its equally resplendent company. As he had feared, the Planters was thronged, even on such a night.

His gray-eyed glance swept the room, quick and eager, losing some of its hope as he made sure that those for whom he looked were not yet here. Convinced of that, he made a more leisurely survey, removing his hat and raincoat.

The Planters House was alive, gay and roaring

with life; bubbling with a false spirit of bravado which sought, not too successfully, to hide the feeling of tension that gripped the land and particularly the town. This was the spring of '64, and there had been the same quivering anxiety when Rawls had made his first visit here in '61.

In those days, St. Louis, a Southern city and proudly conscious of the fact, had been supremely conscious of its destiny in the years ahead. Then as now it had been garrisoned by men in blue, soldiers whom the citizens regarded as interlopers, almost as foreigners.

But in those days, which now seemed so far off, the city had suffered the indignity with confidence that its thralldom would not last long. Everyone had assured Denny Rawls, then, that the Yankees would quickly be swept from the town, as from every other bit of Southern soil.

Now, after three more years of war, that was a hope deferred and grown dim. St. Louis was more firmly in the hands of the North, and tensions had increased with the years. Captive it might be, but St. Louis was still a rebel city at heart, a seething hotbed of rebellion.

Rawls shrugged, undisturbed. You could find plenty of sympathizers for the Confederacy in places other than here, and he accepted the situation as it was. Despite his own sympathies, he could see much to be said on both sides. Though as for St. Louis, he hadn't liked it on his first visit, and he cared even less for it on this his second call.

It was a splendid city, of a hundred and sixty thousand population, and bulging at the seams with the strains of war. That was the trouble. To a man reared on the upper reaches of the Missouri, any place with more than a hundred people in it seemed overcrowded.

The two men from the other carriage had entered the room, coming unobtrusively through a side door. They moved to the bar, not far from where he stood. Rawls gave them a passing glance, noting the chunky beefiness of Sherwood, his pock-marked face and unconscious posturing; the peculiar yellow-red of Taber's hair, hanging overlong beneath his sodden hat, held his attention briefly. The pair looked as out of place in this room as he felt. Then his survey checked at a table in the center of the room.

A woman sat alone, as if waiting for someone. She was young, with generous color in her cheeks, and for the moment she was frowning at a menu, which gave Rawls an opportunity to study her unobserved.

She was outstanding in this gay company which filled The Planters—as she would be anywhere. It was not her beauty, for her nose was a shade too big, her mouth too generous. But there was a striking quality about her which Rawls felt as clearly as the rising heat waves above a stove in a chilly room. Her hair was like ripe wheat, the golden grains bursting through the heads, the sky-blue of June in her eyes.

Suddenly she looked up, and her searching gaze met and tangled with his own and held. It was a straightforward and direct look on her part, like that of a man. Almost it seemed to Rawls that there was a message, a mute appeal, in her eyes, as though she fought a growing unease or apprehension. The Planters, despite its cosmopolitan reputation, seemed scarcely the place for an unattended woman at such an hour.

But that was none of his business, Rawls reminded himself, his glance again roving. And when it came to that, why didn't his own party get here?

He made a second survey of the room, quite unconscious of the eyes, furtive or frankly interested, which compassed him in turn. Many were feminine, turned brightly if briefly speculative. It did not occur to Rawls that he was an impressive figure of a man. The mark of the upper river was upon him, the stamp of far places.

His glance went back to the other table as though drawn, and to his surprise the girl smiled and beckoned. Even then he was conscious of an underlying timidity that belied the apparent boldness of the action. He had the sudden feeling that she felt as out of place here as he did.

The two men who had entered were watching him closely, but Rawls did not notice. He crossed to the table, bowing.

"If I can be of any service—" he began.

Her bodice rose and fell with the hurry of her breath, and her voice had an oddly breathless quality.

"Aren't you Captain Rawls?" she asked. "I hope you won't think me presumptuous, but I was told that you might be coming here this evening, so I —I came in hopes of seeing you. On business," she added quickly.

Her lips were smiling, but her eyes pleaded for understanding at this outrage to the conventions. Rawls bowed again, and slid into the chair opposite her, as though this had been a prearranged meeting.

"Yes, I'm Denny Rawls," he said. "But you have the advantage of me—"

"I know. Thank you for being so understanding. I'll explain." She hesitated for a moment, biting her lip with strong, even teeth, wondering how much she could tell him, sensing what his reaction must be, feeling already that it was a hopeless task that she had set herself. Then she plunged ahead.

"I'm Kathleen Garrison, and I'm looking for a man who knows the upper river, to captain my boat. It's not really mine, of course, but my brother's. He and my father purchased it, since it's almost impossible to charter any river craft. It's here in St. Louis—the *Varina*. With a cargo of supplies for Fort Benton. My brother is at Virginia City."

Part of it was becoming clear. Gold had been found at Virginia City in Montana Territory the previous summer—one of the richest strikes in the history of the country.

Suddenly she smiled, and this time the smile was in her eyes as well as on her lips. Rawls felt his interest quickening.

"It's terribly important," she said. "For the *Varina* to get there, that is. So it's necessary that I hire the best captain and pilot obtainable, and when I heard that you were in town and would be coming here, I came at once. Everyone assures me that you, Captain Rawls, know the rivers in that country better than any other man alive."

"I'm afraid somebody overrates me," Rawls murmured, conscious of his own quickening interest.

"I've heard too much about you to think that. I'm not exactly a tenderfoot when it comes to river boats or streams, and I know enough to realize how important it is to have the right man in charge. To have a competent man whom I can trust. I want to get the *Varina* started up the river as soon as possible. Would you be interested in taking her, Captain Rawls?"

There was far more than the words themselves. Her eagerness, a hidden sense of excitement that she could not quite hide, both impelled and intrigued him. Under any other circumstances and at any other time, he would have been more than interested. Rawls knew a moment of genuine regret. Despite the fact that he had come here to meet his fiancée, that his whole being was atingle with the thought of seeing her again, Kathleen Garrison was a woman to excite any man. She seemed so genuine, her need so real, that he would have liked to help her. But it was, of course, out of the question. He had received strong hints that tonight he would receive another offer, one so attractive that anything else was unthinkable.

Suddenly his face lighted, quickening to eagerness. Those for whom he had been waiting had finally entered the room, were moving toward a table. They hadn't seen him yet, in the crowded dining hall. There was Astrid, looking even more beautiful than he remembered. Astrid and her father—

Then he saw that there was a third member in the party, another man, and his eyes clouded with disappointment. He hadn't expected anyone else tonight, and the way this other man was smiling and talking to Astrid was a sight scarcely pleasing to a man eager to see his sweetheart. She had sent word that she and her father, Lomax McQuestion, would meet him here, the message changing his plan for going straight to her house upon his arrival in the city. But she had said nothing about a third member of the party.

Still, this other man was more than likely a business acquaintance of McQuestion's, for this meeting was to be partly business as well as social.

He was recalled by the look on Kathleen Garrison's face. She flushed painfully.

"I'm sorry. Were you waiting for them?"

"As a matter of fact, I was," Rawls said, and felt regret. His eagerness to reach the other table was not diminished, but had it been possible he would have liked to help her. "I'd like to be of assistance to you, Miss Garrison," he added. "But, as a matter of fact, I won't be free for anything such as you suggest, flattering as the offer sounds. Surely you can find some other man to captain your boat?"

"I don't know who," she said, and he saw the disappointment in her eyes. "I had so hoped that you would be available. But I don't want to detain you—" She hesitated, wondering how far she dared go. All that she had told him had been true, but it was only a part of the whole. If she could only tell him the full truth, save him somehow from that scheming little hussy at the other table—

Her hope had lain in the fact that her offer must be attractive, but that was not enough. Disturbingly she was conscious that her disappointment was not entirely because she would not be able to acquire his competent services. Now that she had seen him, a part of her interest was more personal.

But to tell him the truth, which she had so

unwittingly stumbled upon, would only antagonize him, with no possibility of doing any good. He simply wouldn't believe her. Something of desperation was in her face, and Rawls sensed it without understanding the reason. She was alone and in desperate need of help. He understood something of that, because he'd felt the same when first he came to this roaring city, where everything was strange.

"I'd really like to help you, if I knew of anyone," he said sincerely. "But I'm not at home, here on the lower river. I feel as out of place as an alley cat in a drawing room—"

Astrid McQuestion caught sight of him, across the crowded room, and he saw her stiffen, caught the glances sent his way by the two men of the party. Aware that his face was reddening, Rawls had the feeling of a small boy caught in mischief, and his resentment grew. Though completely innocent, this meeting might be hard to explain. Kathleen seemed to understand, and there was a resignation in her eyes which he misinterpreted.

"Thank you, Captain," she said. "It's been a pleasure to meet you, but I won't detain you, now. If for any reason you should change your mind, let me know."

"If I should, I certainly will, and I hope you

have luck in finding a good man," Rawls agreed,
getting to his feet. It wasn't what he wanted to
say, sounding both perfunctory and abrupt, and
somehow he felt guilty at leaving her this way,
when she so obviously was in need of advice and
help. Discomfited, he turned hastily, and staggered at the impact of a knobby shoulder. The
collision swung him half around, so that he
jolted the corner of the table, upsetting a bowl of
soup that had just been placed in front of Kathleen.

She looked up, startled, and again he saw the
concern in her eyes, though not for the spilled
soup. But he had only an instant for that. The
beefy man with the pock-marked face had jolted
him, and he spoke now, his reedy voice truculent.

"Better look where you're going, Mister—or
are you so drunk you can't tell?"

Anger boiled in Rawls. He had been about to
murmur an apology; now he saw in amazement
that this encounter had not been an accident but
was deliberate, that they intended to pursue it.
The taller man with the odd-colored hair crowded
against Kathleen's chair, almost upsetting the
table.

"Careful what you're about!" Rawls snapped. "Or are *you* drunk?"

"You'n your lady friend think you're too good to 'sociate with us, eh?" That was not too much liquor speaking. For some unknown reason, they were deliberately trying to force a quarrel on him. His perceptions quickening, Rawls saw the pattern. The table would be shoved against him, while the beefy man lunged to catch him off-balance. Momentarily he wondered if this could be a put-up job, in which Kathleen Garrison had some part. As quickly he dismissed that notion, seeing the mounting distress in her eyes. But the pair were already starting their maneuver.

Their mistake lay in being slow and clumsy. Rawls resented interference, particularly at this time, and he was doubly angry that Kathleen should be an innocent victim. He swung about quickly. Onlookers, attracted by the altercation, scarcely had time to see, so smoothly was it done. His long arms reached, his fingers closed on coat collars. With the powerful, precise motions of a nutcracker, Rawls swept the two men together, jerking the taller one around the edge of the table in the process. The crack of skulls was audible throughout the room.

Waiters came hurrying, attracted by the disturbance. As if dusting off his hands, Rawls shoved the groggy trouble-makers into their arms.

"These fellows appear to be drunk," he said, and turned to bow again to Kathleen Garrison.

"I deeply regret this incident, Miss Garrison. You must permit me to pay for the damage to your dress."

"Oh no, not at all. It's quite all right, hardly touched me. And it wasn't your fault, Captain Rawls."

An apologetic waiter was already changing the cloth. There was a hint of laughter in the girl's eyes, driving out the trouble, an added touch of color in cheeks which had no need for it. She had enjoyed the whole incident and his manner of dealing with the men as much as he had, and Rawls had to admit that the episode had relieved a lot of tension that had been building in him.

"I hope we may meet again, Captain," she added. "Under less hectic circumstances."

"I echo the wish," he agreed, but now he was doubly anxious to reach the other table. Bowing again, he turned and resumed his way, uncomfortably conscious that every eye in the room was upon him.

By the time he reached the far side of the room, he had regained his composure, but he was more rigidly erect and carefully precise than he had intended.

"Astrid!" he said, stooping above her chair and taking her hand in both of his for a moment, conscious of how small it was, how surprisingly soft. She was a girl with hair to rival a raven's wing, almost tiny beside her father, and because she had been the first woman in his life, he was breathlessly unsure of himself when with her, amazed at the witchery which could dwell in a woman's smile, the mystery of a woman's kiss.

"It's good to see you again," he added. "I'm sorry for the ruckus," he explained, and turned to shake hands with Lomax McQuestion, who, for all his broadcloth, gave the furry impression of a bear that had blundered upon a picnic.

"Ruckus, was it, Denny?" McQuestion chuckled, in a voice which seemed to rumble up from the toes of his shoes. "Sure and you handled it like you was brushin' a fly off your coat. If that pair was lookin' for trouble, they sure got more'n they bargained for. Denny, you'll have heard of Mark Whirter—both of you being river-boat captains. Mark, this is Denny Rawls. Shake hands with each other."

They obeyed, Rawls with a grave but calculating politeness. Of course he had heard of Mark Whirter. Everyone had. Strangely enough, though both of them had frequented the waterways for years, their paths had never before crossed.

Whirter was as tall as Rawls, wider in the shoulder. The sureness that was in Rawls' gray eyes looked back from his blue ones as contemptuous arrogance, and nothing in his face betrayed that he had taken more than a passing interest in the fracas across the room. He was dressed, like Rawls, in the blue uniform affected by a riverboat captain, though his coat was decorated by a multiplicity of gold braid that Rawls disdained.

"Captain Whirter came along, tonight, partly as an old friend of the family, partly on business," McQuestion explained, when they were seated. Whirter was beside Astrid, with an officious familiarity which Rawls, across from her, resented. But she gave him a smile which made the room warm again.

"Who is your friend at the other table, Denny?" she asked teasingly. "She's very beautiful—and lonely looking. I think she was disappointed that you didn't stay."

Rawls glanced across the room, conscious of his own flush, of a lack in his manners. Kathleen

Garrison had come here alone, braving convention, to see him, to offer him a job, and he'd been barely courteous. Since Whirter was making a third at this table, the polite thing to do would be to invite her over. And perhaps McQuestion would have some helpful suggestion.

But the other table was empty. She hadn't lingered, which was scarcely to be wondered at. Irritation edged his voice.

"Not my friend," Rawls denied. "Those hoodlums merely bumped into her table."

"But she seemed to know you," Astrid persisted, her voice like tinkling honey, if such a thing was possible. "And I think she was disappointed. I'm afraid you're a flirt, Denny."

Rawls did not reply. He was conscious of disappointment that Kathleen was gone, suddenly angry with everyone—those interfering troublemakers, Mark Whirter, himself—even Astrid. Nothing was working out tonight as he had anticipated.

It had been only a week since he'd seen Astrid, but it had stretched like years. That had been a hundred miles up the Missouri, and theirs had been a whirlwind courtship in the preceding days. It had lasted just three weeks—three of the most soul-shaking weeks that he had ever dreamed of. Perhaps he had swept her off her feet with his ardency, just as her sun-kissed beauty, from a winter spent at Memphis, had worked change in him.

One evening, under a bright wing of moon, she'd given him her promise. The next day he'd been called to duty and she had started the return journey. In the days between, he had lived for this next meeting, when he would again be able to hold her in his arms. Certainly *he* hadn't intended for it to be in so public a place, or with a friend of the family along. It was bad enough to have Lomax McQuestion for chaperon.

But Astrid had made the arrangements, and there had been nothing for him to do but accept with as good grace as possible. There had been a scrawled postscript to her note, from Lomax McQuestion, saying that he wanted to talk over some urgent business, as he understood that his prospective son-in-law was now free for a new enterprise. The note had hinted that it entailed the command of the best river packet in the McQuestion fleet.

That had been a pleasurable thrill, for it conveyed a tacit acceptance of his new status, and the McQuestion boats were the pride of the rivers. This was the first time that Rawls had met

McQuestion since Astrid had agreed to marry him. The second time that they had ever met, for that matter.

But now he knew a moment of wonder that such a man as McQuestion could be father to a girl like Astrid. She was as slender and fragile as a reed. McQuestion, by contrast, was a bear of a man, stubby, always smoking a black pipe, always in need of a shave. Though he was dressed for the occasion tonight, clothes could not change him, and he looked like one of the stevedores on his own boats. But looks could be deceiving, for Lomax McQuestion was a name to conjure with here in St. Louis, or anywhere along the river.

Astrid had written that her father had raised no objections to their engagement. That was fair of him, for while Denny Rawls was also a well-known name on the river, certainly he had little to offer a girl in the way of material things.

"You seemed to be limping, Denny," Astrid commented, breaking a silence in danger of becoming strained. "Or did I imagine it?"

Rawls shrugged in light dismissal. "That's from a Minie ball in my foot, a few months back," he explained. "It only bothers me in weather like this. In a way, it's a good thing. I can't march so well now, which is why I'm out of the Army. At first, I was disappointed. But the war, as I see it, is pretty well over. It's only a matter of time, now. This way, I can get back on the river, and that's what I like."

He was conscious of the sudden sharp scrutiny in the eyes of all three, of the hush of attention from those at neighboring tables as he gave his opinion. St. Louis was still a Southern city at heart.

"So that's your opinion, is it—that the war's about ended?" Whirter demanded, and there was a truculent note to his voice. "I'm afraid you're optimistic, sir."

"Maybe." Rawls shrugged again. "In any case, it seems to be over for me."

"That's what we want to talk to you about," McQuestion boomed. "Maybe that Minie ball is a lucky break for both of us. Good men who know the river—especially the upper Big Muddy—are mighty scarce these days. I've a boat I want to send to Fort Benton, and I figured it was a stroke of luck about you, Denny, my boy. You have both a captain's license and a pilot's, I know."

Eagerness crept back into Rawls. One event after another had kept him on the lower reaches of the river too long. To get back to Benton would be like returning home.

"There's nothing I'd like better, sir, if I can serve you," he admitted.

"Fine. That's the sort of answer I like. As you know, they've been making some rich gold strikes up that way of late. They say that the ones at Virginia City and Alder Gulch are among the richest ever found anywhere. So I figure that a cargo of supplies delivered at Benton will be worth a fortune. The *Astrid* is ready to take on a load tomorrow, then start the next morning. All that's been lacking is a man who knows the upper river, a man I can depend on to handle her."

Rawls knew what he meant. The Big Muddy was always a treacherous stream for a river boat. Filled with hidden sawyers, constantly shifting sand bars, changing banks, and tricky currents, it was one of the most difficult of all navigable streams, even in normal times. And these times were far from ordinary.

All the way along the Missouri now were men who felt, in one respect at least, as he believed— that the South was losing the war, and that it was only a question of time, and not too much of that, until the end of the struggle. But many of them, unlike himself, sympathized with the cause of the Confederacy. A lot of them hoped passionately for some miracle that would give the South a new lease on life, and they were ready to do anything they could to hinder the Yankees. Many of their acts were contingent on the principle that enough pinpricks could mount up to an aggravation that might prove a serious diversion.

That attitude often meant trouble for boats carrying supplies on the river. In addition, there was the more ominous threat of Indian trouble. Red Cloud and his warriors were on the warpath, and a smouldering brand might burst at any time into a conflagration to sweep across a thousand miles of mountain and prairie. Caught in its wash would be the river and any who traveled it.

"Can you be ready to take over tomorrow, get loaded and start the next morning?" McQuestion probed. "I'll make it worth your while, boy. And every day counts now, as no man will understand better than yourself."

Mountain snows were melting, feeding the smaller streams which in turn emptied into the Madison, the Gallatin, the Jefferson, the Marias, the Milk, the Yellowstone—feeders for the upper Missouri. The time to travel was at the crest of these high waters.

Rawls hesitated, torn between desires. He had hoped for several days, perhaps weeks, to be spent here with Astrid. That would be out of the

question if he took this job. A snatched hour or
so during the next day, perhaps—then he would
be gone, for a period of months.

But if he made a successful trip, the profits
would be substantial. McQuestion would hardly
be niggardly with his future son-in-law. He looked
at Astrid, saw her eager nod, and made up his
mind.

"If you say tomorrow, tomorrow it is," he
agreed.

From then on, the conversation concerned itself mostly with business, leaving Rawls opportunity for only an occasional word with Astrid.
Indeed, while McQuestion talked to him, Whirter talked to her, so that much of the time she
seemed to forget Denny's existence. Rawls was
conscious of a growing feeling of jealousy and dislike for his fellow-captain. Didn't Whirter know
that they were engaged, almost their first time together since then, in fact? Astrid, at least, should
remember.

In the back of his mind, he mulled over what
he knew concerning Mark Whirter. It was a
name famous on the lower river, as Denny's was
on the upper Missouri. Whirter was known as
"Lucky Mark." He was supposed to be a captain

in the Army of the United States, but tonight he wasn't in uniform.

During the course of the meal, Whirter dropped a remark that seemed to explain his present status. Apparently he was serving as some sort of special agent for the Government.

All that Rawls wanted of Whirter was less of him. But he was given no chance to see Astrid alone. Though making no direct promise, she hinted that tomorrow might be different.

Hiding his disappointment, Rawls accompanied the McQuestions to their carriage. It was still raining, a blustering wind making the night doubly disagreeable. As soon as the carriage was out of sight, Whirter said a curt goodbye and disappeared.

He had taken only a few steps when Taber and Sherwood accosted him. Whirter was in no pleasant mood. He surveyed them caustically.

"Well, what do you want now?" he demanded.

"How about our pay?" Sherwood asked. "We was to be paid—"

"If you made a fool out of him!" Whirter snapped. "But it was the other way around. He made fools of the pair of you. Go to the devil!"

"But we got a pair of headaches—"

"Serves you right! Too bad he didn't crack your thick skulls for you. I don't pay for bungling." He turned impatiently away, took half a dozen steps, and swung back. "However, I'll have work for you in the morning," he added. "A summer of it, in fact. And if you do a good job, you'll get a fat bonus!"

Chapter Two

Kathleen Garrison awoke to the fragrance of coffee, and for a moment it was sufficient to dispel the thoughts which had been with her when sleep overtook her. She smiled and shook her head reprovingly at Narcissus, who, black face abeam, was bringing a tastefully arranged tray to her bedside.

"What's the meaning of this, Narcissus?" she demanded. "Breakfast in bed! Are you trying to spoil me?"

"No'm, nothin' like that, Miss Kathleen," Narcissus denied. "I'm jus' a doing three things. Helpin' to start yo' day right an' drive away the troubles. Expressin' a little o' the depreciation I feel, me havin' been free all my bawn days and wukkin' fo' wages, thanks to yo' daddy, while those other niggahs is just gettin' free now, thanks to Abe Lincoln. An' lastly, but not least, yo' de-servin' of somethin' special while yo' can get it.

Times ahead ain' goin' be easy. I done read the tea leaves."

"What do you mean?" Narcissus called it reading tea leaves, but it was more than that, as she had demonstrated on former occasions. There were those who called it black magic, a jungle power passed on to her from her freeborn grandmother, later enslaved but possessing an untamed heart to the end.

"They's trouble ahead," Narcissus said shortly, and refused to elaborate. "An' yo' bein' yo'self, an' stubborn as yo' daddy was, ain' no need to argue with yo' or agin' fate. So drink yo' coffee an' enjoy it while yo' can, chile."

Kathleen did not resent this, though Narcissus was her senior by less than a year. She sipped thoughtfully, munching at her toast, reviewing the events of the previous evening.

"How sure are you of what you told me yesterday—about Astrid McQuestion?" she demanded sharply.

"Plenty sure," Narcissus retorted promptly. "Us river-farin' families wag our tongues together, an' Comfort been maid to Miss McQuestion two years, an' she don't like her no little bit. She see Cap'n Rawls when he co'tin' Miss Astrid, an' she lak' him. Say he treat her jus' like she a person an' not just a cullud niggah. It make her mad, hearin' Miss Astrid gigglin' an' tellin' how she makin' a plumb fool out of him. Cose, he's that head-over-heels crazy 'bout that gal, he blind as a new-bawn kitten. Can't see the claws she hide in that soft fur.''

Kathleen nodded, forgetting to eat. That was only servants' gossip, but, knowing Narcissus, she had accepted it, had sought to save Denny Rawls from what impended. But she had failed, and it left her troubled as well as disappointed on her own account.

"I couldn't hire him to captain the *Varina*," she said aloud, speaking half to herself. "And who I'm going to get that will be any good—"

"That reminds me," Narcissus said calmly. "Now yo' had yo' breakfast, better get dressed. They's a man waitin' to see you now. Name of Earnshaw. Claims he's a rivah-boat cap'n."

Kathleen sprang out of bed. "And you've kept him waiting? Why didn't you tell me?"

"Why shouldn't he wait?" Narcissus tossed her head. "He sort of a iffy man, if yo' ask me. Mebby he know the river—mebby. A spider know his business, too, but a fly better watch him. They goin' make a fool of Cap'n Rawls, get him in trouble," she added almost as an afterthought.

"How do you know?"

"I got ways o' seein'. An' Comfort got a tongue, repeatin' what others wag. There goin' be pieces to sweep up, does a person be around with a broom an' dustpan come the right time."

Some of Denny Rawls' gloom lifted the next morning at sight of the *Astrid*. This packet, which Lomax McQuestion had named in honor of his daughter, was a stern-wheeler of light draft, especially built for the shallow waters of the Missouri. She was light and graceful, with all the ornate gingerbread woodwork which was in vogue. A garish river scene was painted on the paddle box. The white lattice railing above the decks lent a deceptively fragile air. Stacks of cordwood were piled on the boiler deck, and Negroes were running about with hand trucks, though somewhat aimlessly.

The Missouri came in here to make junction with its final destiny, sweeping savage and majestic, living up to its name of Big Muddy. A chocolate flood poured against the Mississippi, staining it. Plenty of other boats were here, looking like a pile of snow against the blackness of the water. Side-wheelers, tugs, ferryboats. Furnace doors opened to crimson flares.

The levee and the riprapped riverbanks stretched away from the Riviere des Peres to the northern limits of the ever-expanding city. A four-mile slope of granite blocks rose gradually from the water. At its summit, the levee was piled with produce of many kinds—cordwood, sacks of wheat, bales of cotton. Wagons and drays by the hundreds were stirring to a new day's activity. On the far side of the levee were warehouses, saloons, restaurants, ship chandlers. This was the river, but a more crowded segment of it than Rawls cared about.

The rain had stopped, but the skies still lowered. He picked his way forward to the *Astrid,* observing the slowness with which loading was proceeding. Correctly locating the official in charge, he introduced himself.

"I'm Denny Rawls—captain in command of the *Astrid.* Is anything the matter?"

Some of the sullenness and uncertainty in the man's eyes seemed to lift at his name.

"Captain Rawls, eh?" The shipping official shook hands cordially. "I've heard of you, of course, sir. You say you're in command of the *Astrid?*"

"That's right. I'm taking her to Fort Benton,

with supplies for the new Montana mining camps."

"And from all reports, Captain, you're the man who can do it, if anyone can. Well, that makes it better. If you're in command, I guess everything's in order."

His comments were puzzling, but Rawls put the matter aside as he met his crew and superintended the loading of cargo. His first officer was 'Lias Cannon, a man of whom he had never heard, but that was not surprising, and Cannon seemed competent. He had the look of a driver, a cold-eyed man who appeared to know what he wanted and who would brook few obstacles in getting it. But that did not worry Rawls.

What did worry him was the lack of opportunity to see Astrid. Everything seemed to conspire to keep him away from her. After days apart, he still hadn't held her in his arms, kissed her, or had a single word alone with her! He fought back an uneasy conviction that she could remedy that situation readily enough if she tried. She was the daughter of the owner, and from all reports, Lomax McQuestion would do anything that she asked of him. What man wouldn't, for the matter of that!

It was mid-afternoon when Astrid arrived with

her father, and gaily insisted that he come with them. Rawls needed no urging. Turning the loading over to Cannon, he entered their carriage. But to his increasing disappointment, they were not going to the McQuestion house, on a dominating point at the edge of town, but to another restaurant. There was more business to discuss with her father, and no time alone with Astrid.

"How many passengers do we carry?" Rawls asked, rather absently. "As many as can pile aboard, I suppose?"

McQuestion shook his head. "No passengers, Denny," he said. "No passengers at all." Seeing Rawls' look of surprise, he went on rather hastily: "We have a lot of cargo, and there's trouble on the upper river, from all reports. I figure it's too big a risk, both for them and for us, to be cumbered with them. So no passengers. That will save stopping at every town and farm along the way and the waste of days of time. Also, and mindful of possible trouble, we'll have a bigger crew than usual, just in case."

It sounded plausible the way he put it, though on second thought Rawls wondered. Few boat owners gave much consideration to the safety or welfare of their passengers, and there were always plenty who were eager to secure passage and run the attendant risks. They would pay enough to more than make up for small delays or inconveniences. But that was McQuestion's business, and Rawls dismissed it from his mind.

When he finally returned to the boat, the loading was completed and everything was in readiness for an early start the next morning. Tired, for his foot still bothered him, Rawls went to his own room.

He had been sure that Astrid would be down with her father in the morning to see them off. But again he was mistaken. Neither Astrid nor Lomax McQuestion put in an appearance. Having delayed as long as he could, while mists cleared from the river and the sun came booming out of the east, Rawls gave the order to get under way.

He stared bleakly at the river as they pushed against the current, leaving the city behind. There was a pilot in the pilothouse, slated to handle the packet for the first few days, so for the present Rawls had none of that responsibility. Farther upstream he would have to be pilot as well as captain. What rankled was the hurt, the growing suspicion that something was radically wrong.

Unable to put his finger on what it might

be, he tried to shut his mind to the possibility of disaster. These matters were trivial in themselves, capable of ready explanation. It was better to believe that the reasons would be forthcoming in due course. Which, as a philosophy, failed signally to convince.

His mind returned to his first meeting with Astrid, a few weeks before and a hundred miles up the river. She had bowled him over, swept him off his feet. Considering her beauty, the sweet charm she had shown him, his own feeling was not at all surprising. But that she should feel the same way about him was as bewildering as it was wonderful. Yet love him she had, for she had admitted as much when he had voiced his own feelings.

For days he'd had his head in the clouds, his feet scarcely on a deck. He'd been willing to come to St. Louis again because she would be there.

Soberly he reviewed it now, step by step. The first false note had been struck at The Planters. Why had she changed so completely in a few days? For here in her own town it was as though he talked with a stranger—

Rawls staggered to a violent shock, clutched for support, then sprinted for the deck, as the *Astrid,* shuddering violently, came to a halt. No need to ask what had happened. They had hit a sand bar and were hard aground.

Mark Whirter shifted his position on the carriage cushions, grown hard with the miles, and regarded his somewhat sullen companion with a toleration that amounted to amusement. He had looked forward to this trip, but Astrid had proved a less gay companion than he had anticipated.

"You know," he said suddenly, with a contemptuous disregard for the driver of the carriage and Astrid's maid, who rode beside him. "I believe you fell for your own pretty game, my dear, and got tangled in your own skein. In other words, in making love to Rawls, I think you more than half fell in love with him."

"It wasn't my game!" Astrid flashed. "It was all your idea in the first place!"

Whirter was delighted. He always found her amusing in such a mood, like a cat with claws half unsheathed.

"Then you did succumb to his charms!" he teased.

"I didn't," Astrid denied. "Maybe it's all necessary, but I don't like the way it's being worked!"

There was unnecessary vehemence, born of temper. She felt more deeply than he had guessed, and knowing how explosive she could be on occasion, Whirter was quick to recognize the danger. Better to placate her before any damage was done.

"It was necessary," he agreed promptly. "The only way, in fact. And you've played your part marvelously. Like your father, I'll be everlastingly grateful to you."

Astrid basked in praise, and now she relented somewhat. Essentially a shallow person, her moods were quickly changeable.

"I did rather like my part," she confessed. "And he's nice. That's why I don't like this part. Why is it necessary, Mark?"

"For a lot of reasons," Whirter said grimly. "The main one being that your father faced bankruptcy unless he could ship this cargo upriver for a big profit. And with the port authorities and the Army increasingly suspicious of the McQuestion activities—well, we could never have cleared inspection and gotten the *Astrid* started without Rawls to captain her. His reputation did the trick. They didn't pay any further attention after he took over.

"We had to get a man like him, get him to lend his reputation," Whirter went on. "Ordinarily, he'd have been suspicious too, and wanting to know what cargo he carried. But after a whirl-wind courtship with a girl like you, his mind all bemused with love, and the boat belonging to your father—it worked like a charm. Now we're all set, and the lion's share of the credit goes to you."

"That part is all right," Astrid conceded. "But he—he was rather nice."

"When it comes to making love, how about me?" Whirter leaned forward. "I'll soon make you forget him, my dear."

A quick look around confirmed Rawls' first impression. The *Astrid* was fast aground on a bar. Incredulous, he found the pilot taking it calmly.

"That durned bar's shifted since I was along here last," he confessed. "Took me plumb by surprise."

Rawls choked down the words that rose to his lips. It looked like mighty careless work, but now it was up to him to get the boat off. Inspection revealed that there was no particular damage. But it also confirmed that they were hard and fast aground.

They worked for the remainder of the day, without success. In the morning it was necessary to resort to grasshoppering, and it was past noon before they were back in the current. When finally they sighted Jefferson City, the run had been slow. Rawls had no intention of putting in there. He'd take on fresh fuel farther upstream, he decided, making a quick estimate of the supply that remained and the next stop where more was available.

He stood apart, paying no attention to what went on around him, though now he watched the water closely, no longer relying on the pilot. A man who had failed once could do so again. The thought that hammered in his brain was that it would be months before he could complete this trip and return. Months before he could see Astrid again—

He blinked, his gaze sweeping the shore. Then he looked again. The next instant he was signaling for a swing in to the empty wharf. Astrid and Mark Whirter were waiting there, unbelievable as it seemed.

His heart was thudding wildly. Something must have occurred—some new development which made her want to see him again. That made the world right.

Ordinarily there would have been little chance, traveling overland as they must have done, to overtake the boat at Jefferson City, unless they made a continuous journey by night as well as day, using relays of horses. Still, there was always the possibility of some delay on the river, and if somebody wanted to meet the boat badly enough, they could risk the trip. Since that had happened and Astrid was here, nothing else mattered.

His first reaction dimmed. Why, if she was eager to set everything right, should she choose Mark Whirter for a traveling companion? It had been his presence that had spoiled everything in St. Louis.

Rawls tried to recapture some of his enthusiasm as the *Astrid* was warped in, but it was gone in a new disquiet. He could not put his finger on what was wrong, but things were not as they should be. He had a hunch that he'd glean new information soon. Certainly he had no intention of proceeding upriver until he knew definitely where he stood with Astrid.

A look at their faces as he stepped ashore was not reassuring. Whirter was scowling. Astrid's expression he could not fathom, but it certainly was not that of a woman eager to greet her sweetheart.

"This is a surprise, to see you folks here!" Rawls exclaimed, and strove to make his voice hearty. "But a pleasant one!"

"That I take leave to doubt!" Whirter's tone dripped ice. "Though we'll hope that things are not so bad as they seem. Mr. McQuestion placed his confidence in you, Rawls—and falsity in man or ship I cannot condone!"

Rawls looked from one to the other in growing perplexity. Whatever he had expected, this was not it. Whirter was officious, curt.

"I hope there's some mistake, Captain Rawls," he added. "But from the reports which reached my ears, almost as soon as you had left St. Louis, I have no choice but to take a look on board. As I think you know, I'm a special agent for the Government."

"I don't know what this is all about," Rawls said slowly, "but have your look, by all means." He bit back the remark that was on the end of his tongue, that there was a fishy smell about this whole proceeding.

But why? Astrid had agreed to marry him. Lomax McQuestion had appeared to approve to the extent of giving him command of this packet. Would they be involved in a plot against him? It seemed preposterous, but his unease was giving way to concern as he followed them back on board. The crew were watching, and it struck him that they did not appear puzzled or even surprised.

He intercepted a glance between Cannon and Whirter—a quick look filled with complete understanding.

Whirter went ahead, Astrid a couple of steps behind him. Both ignored him, as he followed them down into the hold.

The cargo was there—boxes and barrels neatly stacked, needed articles for Fort Benton and the wild frontier beyond. Mining tools, general hardware and supplies such as would be particularly useful in a new land. Staples in foods, bolts of canvas, calico and other dry goods. He had supervised loading part of it himself, and the boxes were plainly marked as to contents.

It was apparent that Whirter knew what he was looking for and where to find it. He wasted no time in play-acting. His glance roved over some of the pile, ignoring much of it. Then he pulled out a box marked pickaxes and ripped the cover boards off. That had been loaded, Rawls knew, while he'd been absent with the McQuestions during the afternoon.

Inside, instead of pick heads, were rifles. Whirter lifted one out. It was an Indian carbine, the Plains gun, a .50 caliber with Maynard tape lock. An accurate, hard-hitting weapon.

No one spoke. Whirter chose two other boxes,

apparently at random, and opened them. Their contents were the same.

"Perhaps you can explain this, Captain?" he suggested. "How it happens that you're carrying contraband, instead of your supposed cargo? We'd like to know."

"So would I!" Astrid exclaimed. "Contraband, and aboard a boat of Father's! There has never been any taint in connection with the McQuestion line—up to now!"

The words had a false ring. Rawls had loved Astrid for herself, not for her father's money, and in spite of ugly whisperings that he had heard of Lomax McQuestion across the years, particularly the war years. Now his mind, shocked for a moment, was racing.

The authorities in St. Louis had been more than wary of the *Astrid* and its cargo. It was his own reputation as a riverman and a patriot of unimpeachable integrity that had allayed those suspicions and made perfunctory acceptance of the cargo a matter of routine. Knowing his record, they had been convinced that, if he was taking this boat to Fort Benton, everything was as it should be.

This was a time of war. Whether these rifles were intended for sympathizers with the Confederate cause, somewhere along the way, or for Indians—such as Red Cloud's band—in either case they were contraband. Having them on board in defiance of regulations amounted virtually to treason.

He was captain, and his was the responsibility. The fact that he had been called away by Astrid and her father while the contraband was being loaded did not absolve him of that responsibility.

Because he loved Astrid, he'd taken everything on faith. But the evidence was shaping up past doubting. Lomax McQuestion, aided by his daughter, had worked this trick deliberately. And Mark Whirter was hand in glove with them. What the scheme amounted to, how it would be handled now, was still obscure but no longer to be questioned.

"I suppose you have an explanation?" Whirter prodded. "Though I warn you, sir, it had better be a good one—a *very* good one!"

"Oh, Denny—Denny, I didn't think you'd do such a thing!" Astrid flung at him accusingly.

Play-acting! Their whole headlong romance, in which she had fairly flung herself at him, had been play-acting, for this purpose. He was beginning to see, and though one part of him was furiously angry, he managed a shrug of cool detachment.

"I'd like to know the explanation, too," he said. "I'm beginning, Mr. Whirter, to be impressed by the cleverness, the trickery, and the complete lack of scruple which is becoming so manifest!"

Whirter had the grace to color. Then, angry at himself, he roared like an angry grizzly.

"So you don't even deny it!" he shouted. "Not that it would do any good, in the face of the evidence! I've no use for double-crossers, and even less for traitors! As agent for Lomax McQuestion, you're fired. Mr. Cannon, heave this stuff overboard, at once!" He swung to Astrid, standing as though stunned.

"There's one lucky thing about this, my dear. That we found out what sort he was, in time. You're well rid of him."

"Yes." Astrid's voice was little above a whisper. Her face showed white and strained. She was tugging at the ring on her finger, the one Rawls had given her, and which had been his mother's. Now she thrust it into his hand, not looking at him. Then she was almost running, back on deck and across to the dock.

Rawls watched her go, and something deep inside him hurt, but the other part, the bystander, observed with a cynical sureness that this was only more acting. She had been putting on an act from the first.

It was the bitterness of that knowledge that dulled the other implications to a lesser ache. There could be no doubt as to the outcome of this. He was ruined. The news would spread all up and down the river, and if he escaped a long term in prison, he would still be an outcast, his name forever blackened.

The pilot had deliberately grounded the *Astrid* to cause sufficient delay for Astrid and Whirter to overtake her here, and they had made that trip with the foreknowledge that they would arrive in time, and of what they would find. Every detail of the plot fitted.

But why? Probably they had needed him to get this boat out of St. Louis with its contraband cargo. But, once on the river, why stage this public show here, deliberately to ruin him?

The answer to that, of course, was Mart Whirter. Whirter was in love with Astrid, and wildly jealous. Apparently the first part of the scheme had succeeded too well to suit him. Perhaps As-

trid, too, had been duped. Maybe she was innocent, being used as he had been. This had been
worked to look black against him.

Cannon was moving briskly, bawling for the
crew, lugging boxes to the deck and sending
them over the side with a splash. All this planned
readiness was doubly damning. Rawls went
ashore, his mind busy with the implications.

"Am I to understand that I'm under arrest?"
he demanded.

Whirter frowned. A small crowd had collected,
attracted by the arrival of a boat and the unusual
spectacle of boxes of cargo being heaved over the
side.

"I should arrest you, by rights," Whirter retorted. "Running contraband guns is nothing
less than treason in such times as these. But we
were lucky enough to catch you in time to avert
any damage. And I have an idea that you'll cause
no more trouble from here on out." He hesitated, choosing his words carefully. "By rights, I
should take you back to stand trial. But there are
other and more important matters which require
my attention. I'm afraid I'll just have to let you
go, much as I dislike to."

"The devil you will!" Rawls said roughly.

"Since you've gone this far, I demand that you take me back and press your charges! I have a right to a trial!"

"There's not the slightest question as to what would happen to you, in event of trial," Whirter retorted. "You've made your bluff, and now you can be mighty glad that I have more important matters to attend to."

He swung abruptly and was lost in the crowd, giving Rawls no further opportunity to protest. But he had spoken loudly enough for the bystanders to hear. This was branding him a traitor. The news would spread fast, not alone in town, but all up and down the river.

Aware of the scornful glances cast his way, Rawls turned, moving blindly, away from the waterfront. Whirter had said enough that he'd be finished on the river. He had been captain of a McQuestion packet, and had been fired in disgrace. The full and embellished story of double-cross and treason would spread. Though he might be one of the best captains, and the most skillful pilot of the upper river, no one would hire him again in any capacity—not even as a deck hand.

Rawls stopped, swinging his head with the uneasy motion of a buffalo bull. Then he turned and started to tramp back, aware that he had walked for miles into the country. They'd gone too far—too damned far! This had a stink worse than skunk, and cried of frame-up from the first.

He wouldn't let Whirter get away with it! If the man was a Federal agent, as he claimed, then he'd insist on arrest and trial. If found guilty and hanged, he'd be no worse off than now. Death would be preferable to living under such a stigma.

But before a duly constituted tribunal he'd have some things to say and questions to ask that might prove embarrassing to Whirter and McQuestion. Small wonder that Whirter preferred just to get him in bad, then duck out from under.

The distance stretched wearily. By the time he returned, dusk was closing over the river, so that only the silver sheen of it made a long track against the blacker fields and wooded slopes stretching beyond. He reached the dock and stared in surprise. The *Astrid* was gone.

Somehow he hadn't forseen such a development. If her cargo was to be thrown overboard, she would be busy for hours. Also, she was without a captain. It would take time to make fresh arrangements.

Yet she was gone, completely out of sight. And that seemed of a piece with the rest of the pattern, all planned in advance.

He encountered a bystander, dim in the gloom, and questioned him.

"Oh, that boat that put in here? Durned queer thing. She wasn't here more'n a half-hour, altogether. Then she tuk out upriver again, crowdin' her b'ilers close to bustin', looked like to me. Black smoke pourin' from her stacks. Musta been puttin' oil on the wood."

Upriver! Rawls had supposed that she would turn back for St. Louis. Though now that he was beginning really to understand, he knew that in that assumption he had also been wrong. The shortness of the stop argued that scarcely anything had been thrown away—only a bit for show.

"How could she go on without a captain?" he asked.

"How? Mister, all I know is what happened. They tell me that Cap'n Whirter took over. And she had the owner on board, too, McQuestion. He come scootin' in here like he was in a hurry. Reckon he could captain her in a pinch, or pilot her, either one. Guess they won't be lackin' none that way."

Chapter Three

Mark Whirter's gloating triumph at the manner in which he had disposed of a rival was tempered when Lomax McQuestion came on board. It had been Whirter's suggestion that they arrive in two groups and the situation he handled in this fashion, with McQuestion remaining out of sight. McQuestion had been willing.

But fury exploded from the ship owner when he discovered that the *Astrid* was ready to pull out and head upstream, and that Rawls had been disposed of much more completely than he had anticipated.

"Do you mean to say that you set him ashore and he's left the town?" McQuestion roared. "Of all the knot-heads! I supposed that you'd clap him in irons, or at least under arrest, and in the hold!"

"I didn't want to do that," Whirter protested. "He's served our purpose. This way he's disgraced and discredited, which is far better for our purpose—"

"Is it, now? Can you think no farther than this end of the voyage? Who's going to pilot us when we get above Fort Union? What do you know of the upper river, much less of the other streams in that country? Find me a man anywhere that knows those waters half so well as Denny Rawls!"

"I didn't think of that," Whirter confessed, crestfallen. "Though I'm an experienced riverman, as you know——"

"Bosh and poppycock!" McQuestion said rudely. "You're a greatly overrated chump. Here on the lower river you're good enough to get by, with luck. But up there you're only a captain, and that's not enough. But I suppose we'll have to make the best of it, though I didn't figure to be dealing with fools!"

Kathleen Garrison made her decision, one which brought a flutter of excitement to her pulse, though her face betrayed none of it as she studied Jacob Earnshaw and listened to his glibly recited qualifications.

"I have a captain's license, though up to now I've served only as first officer," he admitted, fingering a long chin with bony hand. "But as a pilot I know the Missouri. I understand that's what you want."

His voice was respectful enough, but there was a little secret smile about his mouth which was too calculating for her taste. But he would probably do as well as any man she could get, now.

"Very well, you're hired," she said. "As first officer," she amplified, and watched his over-prominent Adam's apple bulge as he choked down his disappointment.

"You have a captain already, then?" he asked.

"I'll serve as my own captain, for a while at least," Kathleen explained. "I was brought up on the river." Dismissing him with instructions to get the *Varina* loaded and ready to go, she turned to Narcissus, her excitement unhidden.

"I'm following what my dad would have called a hunch," she explained. "But you said that there would be pieces to be swept up—if someone was handy to do it. We're going to Fort Benton too."

Narcissus blinked. "Ain' that kind of sudden? And that's pretty wild country, from all I hear."

"It *is* sudden," Kathleen confessed. "But I can't see any other way. Of course, you don't have to go along, Narcissus. If you don't like the idea—"

"Who says I don' like the notion?" Narcissus demanded indignantly. "Ain' I always gone where yo' is? But this ain' goin' be no tea party, Miss Kathy. Leastwise, if it is, it be one o' those *Boston* tea parties I hear yo' an' yo' frien's discussin' one day. Well, I go pack a dustpan!"

The night was settling more blackly, but the pattern was becoming clearer to Rawls. If the *Astrid* had gone on upstream, with Whirter and McQuestion, it meant that the whole thing had been planned carefully in advance. If the packet had tarried not more than half an hour—he smiled bitterly.

Mark Whirter's order to throw the contraband into the river had been a part of the scheme. Some boxes had been tossed overboard, but if anybody here in Jefferson City cared to go to the trouble of diving for them, or grappling to bring them to the surface, in the hope of securing rifles, they would be disappointed. Those boxes would contain nothing more useful than scrap iron or rock to give them weight.

Whirter claimed to be a Federal agent, but this had a strange sound. A shipload of rifles and ammunition delivered to the Indians or a band of guerilla raiders could cause untold damage. If the border were set aflame, it might require the sending of thousands of soldiers, regular Army men who could ill be spared from the main conflict. But that must be what was planned.

The devilish ingenuity of the scheme was staggering. They'd needed him and his reputation to get the *Astrid* out of St. Louis, but now, if he went to the authorities and told his story, he was so discredited that he would be laughed to scorn. His hands were tied, himself a marked man. Even on the unlikely chance that he could interest someone with authority, the *Astrid* was safely away, and there would be little or no chance of doing anything about it.

He felt trapped, and the feeling was enhanced as the hours wore on. There was no way of telling when another boat might put in at the landing. It might be days or weeks. In any case, the news would have run ahead, and he wouldn't be welcomed, probably not even allowed to set foot on board.

Aside from the boats, there was only one daily stage as a means of communication with the outside world. It would not be along until the middle of the next afternoon.

Driven by hunger, he entered a dingy little restaurant and ordered a meal. He had hoped to go unrecognized, but some bystander saw him and spread the word. A man who had been loitering at an adjoining table got up and spat on the floor. The room was quickly deserted, save for the waiter. He stood, scowling, until Rawls finished his meal, eating as quickly as possible, the food tasteless in his mouth.

He returned to the sheltering dark, his cheeks burning. That was what he was in for now, everywhere he went. The brand put upon him would burn deeper as time went on, and he could say nothing in his own defense.

Outside of town he found a haystack and burrowed into it for the night. Breakfast, in another small restaurant, was almost a repetition of the night before. One man accosted him on the street, begging for trouble. Rawls was hard put to it to keep from giving him what he sought. He went on, cheeks burning, the taunt of cowardice added to the others thrown in his ears. But if he knocked the fellow down, one of two things would happen. Either he'd be thrown into a filthy jail and held for worse things, or, more than likely, lynched.

He had to get away. Yet he felt a curious reluctance to go, as though this drama was not yet played out, that he had a part remaining. Which was ridiculous, with the *Astrid* gone and everyone hostile.

But the notion persisted, so strong as to be a hunch, and in any case he had to wait for the stage. He saw its dust finally, and then, looking toward the river, discerned a smudge above the water—an approaching packet, bound upriver.

Despite himself, his footsteps carried him in that direction. The stage would be gone while he loitered, but time had ceased to have importance, and conditions would be much the same one place as another. The incoming boat drew him like a magnet.

It was a sleek, graceful craft, one which would have as much speed as the *Astrid*. With a swirl of white water it came in, turning toward the dock. As the boat neared the shore and the figures on deck became recognizable, Rawls felt sheer amazement.

She was dressed differently now, but, once seen, Kathleen Garrison was not a girl easily forgotten. And *Varina* was the name on the bow of the boat, flaunted like a battle flag in these days of civil strife. Varina was the name of the wife of Jefferson Davis, President of the Confederacy.

She came nosing in, her paddle wheel churning a froth, smoke coming in little sighing spurts from her stacks. A trim and graceful craft, the *Varina* was a side-wheeler, long and low with a lofty superstructure, one of the floating palaces so much in vogue before the war. He looked to see the cabin deck lined with passengers, but, like the *Astrid,* there seemed to be none on board.

What caught and held his attention was the girl, standing on the texas beside an officer in gold braid. He watched with a feeling of eagerness totally out of proportion to the occasion. Certainly he couldn't presume on their brief acquaintance even to speak to her now. Having heard the news, she would have no more use for him than anyone else. He should move away while opportunity offered. But he stood rooted to the spot, and the feeling that this was a moment of destiny was too strong to down.

The *Varina* was made fast, and Kathleen came ashore, accompanied by the tall officer. All doubt of her intentions was dispelled as she hurried toward him.

"Captain Rawls!" Her voice was warm, excitedly friendly. "This is a piece of luck, finding you here." She turned to the man beside her. "Captain, this is Mr. Earnshaw—my first officer on the *Varina.*"

Rawls inclined his head. He'd heard the name, had observed how smoothly the *Varina* was brought in, and the overlarge crew, similar to that on the *Astrid,* which had jumped to obey orders. But beyond these things, he knew nothing of the man.

"A pleasure," he said, and Earnshaw nodded jerkily.

"I've heard of you, of course, Captain," he agreed drily.

Kathleen's tone was breathless. "I saw you standing here, so we put in at once," she said. "I—I hope that you may have changed your mind—since the other evening."

Rawls eyed her in amazement. She couldn't have heard the story, then. "I appreciate the offer," he said, "but there have been certain developments since then—things which would make it unfair to you for me to accept. Once you have heard the story, you'll understand."

Her face flushed painfully, but her eyes were steady.

"We've heard what happened here," she admitted. "But knowing you, Captain Rawls, I'm sure there's been a mistake. For my part, I'm certain of it. The *Varina* is bound for Fort Benton. I've been acting as my own captain this far, but if you will assume command, I shall feel that what has been an ill wind for you was a good one for me."

It was a graceful speech, the sincerity of which could not be mistaken. Rawls saw amazement, followed by quick fury, in Earnshaw's eyes, but after a moment the man had control of himself, and as Rawls glanced inquiringly at him, Earnshaw seconded his employer.

"Don't hesitate on my account," he said. "In these waters I feel myself competent to take charge, but the upper river would be a different story. Up that way I wouldn't want to risk a valuable cargo, to say nothing of the *Varina*."

His frankness was disarming, but somehow it didn't quite ring true. Kathleen gave a quick sidewise glance which seemed to indicate that this humbleness on Earnshaw's part was new to her.

"Are you sure that you're not just being sorry for me?" Rawls asked.

"The news, the way it reached my ears, sounded dreadful," she said frankly, and wished that she might tell him why she disbelieved it—that through servants' gossip she had known in advance of a plan to use him and then wreck him, cast him aside "like dirt to be swept up," as Narcissus had so graphically put it. But of course she couldn't explain, though the working-out of the scheme had strengthened her own belief in this man who had been victimized.

"But I don't believe it," she added. "You can help me. If this will perhaps help you to clear yourself, then it will be to our mutual advantage. Will you come?"

"I'll come," Rawls agreed. "And thank you." Turning, he followed her aboard. This was luck, such as he had not expected. It would be both triumph and revenge to bring the *Varina* and berth her alongside the *Astrid,* at Fort Benton.

At his nod, Earnshaw gave the orders and they cast off again, got under way. Rawls turned to go below, and checked suddenly. Then he leaped, and his fingers closed on a hurrying, furtive figure, twisting the man around. He hadn't been mistaken. This was the taller of the two men who had tried to make a fool of him, that night at The Planters.

Taber twisted in Rawls' grasp, then relaxed sullenly. Having had a demonstration of the power that dwelt in this man's hands, he had no stomach for more.

"Now this is something, finding you here!" Rawls snapped. "I suppose that means that your pardner's somewhere around?"

Taber was saved the need for answering, as Kathleen hurried up, attracted by the commotion. Recognizing his captive, she stared with widening eyes.

"Where—where did he come from?" she gasped. "Why—he's one of those men who were at The Planters—"

"Exactly," Rawls agreed. "And I'm curious about finding him here, too. Talk!" he added to Taber.

"There ain't much o' nothin' to tell, Cap'n," Taber whined. "Me and my pard, Sol Sherwood, we just asked for a job, and got it. We sure didn't figure on runnin' into either o' you, beggin' your pardon." He rolled his eyes from Kathleen to Rawls and back. "We're just crew hands, tryin' to do our work. As for that night, we was drunk. Just drunk enough to make trouble, but it won't happen again—no more liquor for either one o' us!"

Rawls let him go. The story was plausible, but he didn't believe it. They had been trouble-makers on shore, and they'd bear watching afloat, but at least forewarned was forearmed. Kathleen was distressed.

"I wonder if he was telling the truth? Somehow, I don't quite believe him."

"Nor I," Rawls agreed. "But if you're willing to give me the benefit of the doubt, I guess I can't do any less with him." He changed the subject abruptly. "Are you planning to go along to Fort Benton?"

"Yes. There's nothing to keep me in St. Louis. I want to see how Bob is getting along, and be sure that he gets this cargo. It's important to both of us. Everything we have is tied up in this trip."

"This is your first trip up the Missouri?"

"Yes. You see, Dad and Bob went upriver a couple of years ago. Due to the war, the family fortunes in shipping were at a low ebb, and they decided to try prospecting. Last year, at Virginia City, they staked a rich claim, then sold it for a good price. With that stake they went into business. It's a wild country, a long way from towns or stores, and Dad had been a small-town merchant at one time. He saw the possibilities in trading, running a store. I guess it turned out to be a bigger gold mine even than a good claim."

"It could easily do that."

"Yes. Anyway, they wanted more supplies. The trouble was to get them there, conditions being as they are. Some are shipped overland, by way of Salt Lake, but that's slow and costly and pretty uncertain. Bob got the idea of buying a boat, since we used to be shipowners, and bringing up a whole cargo for their own use. They purchased the boat through a St. Louis agent, contracted for the cargo, and—and then things commenced to go wrong."

"Yes?" Rawls' voice was sympathetic.

"Dad—was killed. An accident. That's about all I know about it. But it meant that Bob couldn't come down and take charge, as he had planned. He had to stay there, to look after things. So he sent me legal papers and told me to hire a captain. I had hoped to get you, because you know that country. We have flour, beans, molasses, hardware, miners' tools, and so on. You can see now, why I'm glad to have you along. And to answer your question, I'm anxious to see that country."

"It's a beautiful land." Enthusiasm crept into his voice. "Wide, with an endless sky overhead. Off beyond where the boats go, there are the mountains, and that's a totally different country, where the world stands on edge."

"You love it, don't you?"

"Yes. I was born there. My folks were among the first to go that way in a covered wagon. That was back in the days when there was a lot of excitement about getting settlers for the Oregon country, so that it would be populated by Americans and go to the United States. My folks never got that far—not to the real Oregon country. But what they did reach has always suited me. This is a fine time to see the upper Missouri country, with spring advancing as we head north. The only bad thing this year is the threat of Indian trouble."

"I'd as soon risk one kind of war as another," Kathleen said seriously. "Bob had to buy a lot of this stuff on credit, and if this trip is successful, it will pay all our debts and we'll own the *Varina,* and have something ahead. But if anything should happen—"

She left that unfinished, but Rawls understood. River-boating was a hazardous occupation, and many things could happen—bursting boilers, the bottom ripped out of a boat by a sawyer, or other disasters that always lurked around the river.

"They say that you know the Missouri better than any other man," she added. "Do you think it would be safe to run at night, while the moon is full?"

"It's risky, but if you say so, we'll do it," he agreed.

"Then I say so," she nodded. "Time is vital."

That suited him. If they could overtake the *Astrid* . . .

Observation soon convinced him that Earnshaw was an efficient officer. The early moon, nearly at the full, arose just as the sun was setting. The river was wide, and under this thin light they kept running, Rawls at the wheel.

Constant alertness was required. Debris rode the river like a tide, but what they could see wasn't too bad. It was the mass of stuff in and under the water, the invisible bars and sawyers concealed by the coffee-colored floor, which made the real hazard.

As he had estimated, the *Varina* was built for speed, and he was soon satisfied that they could at least match the *Astrid,* mile for mile. It struck him that the wish was illogical. To overtake the *Astrid* short of Benton would be inviting additional trouble for himself. Certainly he didn't want to see Astrid herself again, or any of that crew. But the eagerness persisted.

There was an informality aboard the *Varina* which did not prevail on the regular packets, particularly the floating palaces which in normal times plied the Mississippi. Normally the cabin deck would be lined with passengers, but since there were none on board, extra cargo was stowed wherever possible.

On the *Varina,* as on most boats, a long saloon stretched the length of the boat—rich with costly carpets, glittering chandeliers and handsome furniture, and lined with staterooms on both sides.

The Gentlemen's Cabin in the forepart was reserved for men, while the rear quarter of the saloon, farthest from the boilers, was the Ladies' Cabin, shut off by glass doors. But Kathleen, as owner, made it plain from the start that she would go anywhere and everywhere as the notion took her. She delighted in climbing to the lofty pilothouse which crowned the texas.

The next few days were uneventful, almost an anticlimax to what had gone before. Then, taking an unheralded look at the cargo in the hold, Rawls encountered Sherwood. The fat man had taken pains to keep out of his way, and he tried to skulk unobtrusively to one side, but as the boat lurched in rough water, he staggered and Rawls caught a whiff of his breath. The pair had not been drunk that night in St. Louis, but there was no doubt about Sherwood being drunk now.

"Where did you get it?" Rawls demanded

sternly. There wasn't supposed to be any liquor on board. Kathleen had made that the rule.

"I—I had a bottle," Sherwood whined. "I didn't think it'd make any difference if I—if I took jus' a nip."

"Show me," Rawls commanded, and momentary panic flickered in Sherwood's eyes.

"I finished it an' threw it overboard," he said. "That was all I had."

"You're lying," Rawls retorted. "We'll have a look around."

His suspicions aroused, it wasn't hard to follow his nose to a keg marked vinegar, but which had been broached at the bunghole, and a siphon inserted. One sniff confirmed his certainty that this was whiskey.

And if there was one barrel of whiskey—he eyed the other barrels hidden beneath innocent-looking material. Jerking at a long wooden box to get it out of the way, a board pulled loose. A prickle of apprehension raced along his spine. This box was kin to the one that Mark Whirter had pried open on the *Astrid,* and, like it, it was filled with rifles.

This was too pat to be coincidence, two fast boats heading upriver almost together, both filled with contraband, with cargoes more explosive in these times than dynamite. And this boat was openly called the *Varina!*

But he couldn't accept what seemed so obvious, that Kathleen either knew or could be implicated. They had been clever enough to pull the wool over his eyes, to use him for a tool, and if they could do that with him, it ought not to be more difficult to hoodwink Kathleen, who had certainly not superintended loading the boat.

"Having a look around, Captain?"

Rawls spun about. The usual respect was lacking in Earnshaw's voice, and in one hand he toyed with a revolver. Behind him were not only Sherwood and Taber, but two other members of the crew, and it needed only a glance at their faces to assure Rawls that the crew, like the cargo, had been selected by Earnshaw and would do his bidding.

"So that's the way the wind blows!" Rawls murmured.

Earnshaw nodded affably. "That's the way," he agreed. "A mistake was made at Jefferson City. Lomax McQuestion left instructions for me to rectify it if possible, but that was taken care of by Miss Garrison even before I received his letter. It's the opinion of Mr. McQuestion that your knowledge of the upper river will be of great value."

Rawls shrugged. "Supposing I don't care to co-operate?"

It was Earnshaw's turn to shrug. "That would be unwise. But I don't think you'll be so foolish. It all boils down to the fact that you have no choice."

Chapter Four

"Just what is this all about, Mr. Earnshaw? Please explain yourself!"

Kathleen's voice was crisply incisive, tinged with anger. She was bewitchingly pretty, with hot color staining her cheeks, and Earnshaw seemed fully appreciative of that as he turned about and bowed, half in mockery, half in deference.

"It is as you see, Miss Kathleen. Necessity forces me to assume command of this packet—"

"They loaded her with whiskey and guns," Rawls cut him off. "Which they intend to deliver to customers of their own choosing. Mr. Earnshaw seems to be working for Lomax McQuestion. That's the trouble."

"That's a blunt way of putting it, but it compasses the case adequately," Earnshaw murmured. "We regret the necessity that it had to be your boat that was involved, Miss Kathleen—"

"Miss Garrison to you!" she interrupted icily.

"As you wish. But you will understand that this is a time of war, and the fortunes of war—" His voice held genuine regret.

Kathleen had regained her composure. That she understood the situation was manifest in her next words.

"So you and the crew turn out to be rebels and traitors," she said bitterly, and Earnshaw's pale cheeks flushed.

"Traitors is a somewhat harsh word," he protested. "Like rebels, I consider it undeserved. For my part, I've no particular love for either side in the current senseless conflict. I like to think of myself as a businessman, with the acumen to grasp at opportunity when it presents itself. There is a difference—"

"There is, and I see that I owe honest rebels an apology," Kathleen said scathingly. "You're a renegade, ready to sell your soul to the devil if he'll bid high enough."

That stung. As Earnshaw had revealed, he was a man of some culture and education, and she had pricked him in a tender spot.

"Words," he said, "are instruments of many uses. It may be better if we use them only for necessary communication. It is unfortunate, Miss

Kathleen, that you decided on this journey north, but since you are here, it becomes necessary that you continue with us. Captain Rawls likewise must accompany us, as his knowledge of the river is invaluable. So long as both of you conduct yourselves circumspectly, making no trouble and not attempting to escape, you will be well treated. Should either of you be so ill-advised as to attempt the foolhardy, then whatever measures may be necessary will be adopted."

He turned on his heel and climbed the stairs, pocketing his gun. The others hesitated, then went about their business, leaving Kathleen and Rawls to their own devices. That they would be watched at all times went without saying, but Earnshaw was apparently satisfied that neither could cause serious trouble.

He had said enough to make it plain that he was employed by Lomax McQuestion, and that they would sooner or later make rendezvous with the *Astrid*. The pattern was becoming clear. McQuestion, working with Mark Whirter, had seen the chance to make a big profit if he could manage to get a couple of boatloads of whiskey and guns upriver.

Kathleen's eyes were dark with dismay.

"What are we going to do?" she asked.

Rawls shook his head. "I wish I knew," he said. "So far, I've no ideas."

"It seems to be just the two of us against them," she said thoughtfully. "And those are pretty long odds."

"I'm sorry that you're along—and that it had to be your boat," Rawls said, but she shook her head.

"Don't worry about that part of it. I'm sorry for Bob—but the fortunes of individuals don't count at a time like this. If guns and whiskey are turned over to the Indians, along with what they already have, it can mean horrible death for women and children as well as men, in a hundred isolated settlements. And if the whole border is set aflame—"

Before she could say more, Taber appeared. His manner was officious.

"No plottin' together," he warned. "If you two want to talk, do it on deck, where everybody can see."

And where others could hear. Rawls shrugged, and Kathleen said soberly, "I'm sorry that I got you back into this, after you were safely out of it."

"Don't let that worry you. Right now, I wouldn't be anywhere else by choice."

If that sounded boastful, it was only what he

meant. He'd been used as a cat's-paw, made a fool of, and the thought rankled. Somewhere along the line, there was a score to be evened with Lomax McQuestion, with Mark Whirter, and various lesser individuals.

The next couple of days convinced him that opposition would not be easy. This crew had been hand-picked and carefully planted, and that left just three of them in opposition—Kathleen, Narcissus, and himself. Kathleen had told him of Narcissus' uncanny ability to glimpse the future, though she had refrained from explaining that she had known, via servants' gossip, how he was being led into a trap. Some knowledge was better kept secret.

But Narcissus was unhelpful in this particular situation. The future was black and troubled. Beyond that she could not foresee with certainty.

The *Varina* continued upriver, under the competent direction of Earnshaw, with Rawls increasingly called upon to act as pilot. Since the *Varina* belonged to Kathleen, he was interested in keeping her afloat. It would be a simple matter to rip her bottom out or smash her almost any hour of the day. That would put a serious crimp in the plans of McQuestion, but it would ruin Kathleen and her brother. Worse, they would still be captive to the infuriated crew, provided they escaped destruction when the boat went down.

His first usefulness, aside from piloting, came at Council Bluffs.

"There'll be an inspection here by Army officers," Earnshaw explained. "And under some conditions, it's pretty stringent. So it'll be better if you appear as captain in charge. There's little likelihood that news of your misfortunes will have reached this far, so your say-so will clear us without any trouble."

"You're confident that I'll give such a say-so?" Rawls asked.

"Completely certain, Captain Rawls. Personally, I should regret very much any inconvenience to Miss Garrison, particularly any affront to her person. But in this case you are each more or less a hostage for the good behavior of the other. I trust I make myself clear?"

"Entirely so," Rawls agreed. "I'll do my part."

Word of his disgrace had not reached Council Bluffs, which indicated that the crew of the *Astrid,* still ahead, had been discreet. As Earnshaw had prophesied, his word as captain made the inspection cursory. Meanwhile, each day brought them closer to a rendezvous with destiny.

There would be further inspections at Forts Pierre and Union. Earnshaw seemed unworried about the last, though it was likely to be the most thorough. Fort Pierre was still some distance ahead, and here were stretches where the river made wide loops, almost turning back upon itself. These were treacherous waters, constantly changing with the whims of the river, a pilot's nightmare. Sure knowledge of the channel one day was no guarantee of safety twenty-four hours later. Waters deep and placid one day might be a trap on the next.

Rounding one of these horseshoe bends, they came upon the *Astrid*. She was anchored in a slow-stirring backwater not far from the east shore. A hoary bluff rose above, wooded with tall cottonwoods which shaded the decks of the motionless packet. A stone's throw away a second packet was similarly at anchor, both boats seeming to drowse in the early afternoon sun.

Rawls made out the name on the second boat, *Pride of Kansas*. Passengers as well as crew were grouped on her decks, watching the arrival of the *Varina* with a mounting excitement.

"Now what's going on?" Earnshaw wondered aloud. "There must be trouble."

That was a safe guess, and once the *Varina* was

within shouting distance, it was soon explained. Captain Bryan Dudley, a big man with a foghorn voice, bellowed at them.

"Indians!" he said. "Renegades! At least, they must be led by a renegade. They've got hold of a cannon, somewhere or other. Got it set up on the bank at the Devil's Spin, a couple of miles up-river. You know the place, Rawls. Bad enough under any conditions, and I've never seen it worse, the water's a millrace now. It takes careful going to get past without being caught in the Spin and smashed against the rocks. No choice of a channel. Which brings a boat under point-blank range of that cannon for five minutes. I tried to run it two days ago. They almost sunk me. All that saved us was the speed of the current, which carried us back downstream out of range before they could finish me off. Been making repairs since and trying to figure out what to do."

The *Astrid* had been there for a day and a night, made uneasy at the prospect. The cannon was big enough that one well-placed shot could sink a boat, and it was apparent from Dudley's experience that it was operated by a competent gunner.

With the arrival of the *Varina,* a conference of captains was called. Mark Whirter and Lomax McQuestion came across to the *Varina,* along with Dudley. Earnshaw spoke a cautioning word before they set foot on deck.

"You're in command, Rawls," he said. "But you'll realize that it would be unhealthy for Dudley, as well as you, to suspect that anything was amiss. Besides, this looks like a situation where we should all work together for the common welfare."

Rawls made no promises, but he recognized the force of the argument. Whirter hid a scowl as he set foot on board, but Lomax McQuestion advanced with outstretched hand and booming voice.

"Well, well, Denny, it's good to see you again!" he said. "Sure and if there's one man who knows this country and what to do in it, you're the one! And that's what we all have need of now!"

"That's true," Dudley agreed. "It's a devil of a mess, and so far, we've been able to find no way out. There's a hundred painted devils on the shore if there's one, caperin' and wavin' guns and tomahawks, and if a boat is crippled, they'll swarm aboard."

"And the weather's on their side," McQuestion added gloomily. "It'll be a full week, barring a stormy night, before it'll be a dark-enough night to sneak past without being sunk."

"A week's delay now can mean low water farther up, so that it's risky business whether we'd make Benton at all," Whirter added.

"Aye," Dudley agreed drily. "But who's fool enough to try and take a boat past that cannon on a night so dark they can't see it? Not me, in these waters. It's bad enough by daylight."

The others looked questioningly at Rawls, but he shook his head. "Captain Dudley's right. When they can't see, neither can we. It would be suicide to try."

"Which seems to leave us back where we were," Dudley added. "With the devil on one side and hell on the other."

Lomax McQuestion tugged at his chin. "It sounds bad," he admitted. "But if we stay here, it's ruin for all of us. It was bad for one boat, and risky for two. But now there are three. And we've the best pilot on the river to guide us. I propose that we do what we have to—spend the afternoon laying in a fresh supply of wood, then all three boats run the gauntlet together, tonight. At least a couple of us ought to get through, maybe all three without too much damage. And then the others can give as much help as possible."

"I'm for that," Dudley agreed. "Since it's Hobson's choice."

"And since you've been a casualty already, we'll give you as good a break as possible," McQuestion added smoothly. "Captain Rawls will have to go first with the *Varina,* because he knows the river. We'll follow with the *Astrid,* and you come third in line with the *Pride.* After all," he added, to forestall possible objections on Dudley's part, "it's a gamble, and besides, you carry passengers, and we don't. They deserve the best chance, if there is any."

And so it was agreed.

Preparations went swiftly forward. The actual attempt at running the blockade would be made a little after midnight, a time when the light was tricky, yet sufficiently good for landmarks to be seen. Meanwhile, more wood must be taken aboard, for from here on it would be increasingly difficult to obtain.

There was a woodcutter's lot half a mile upstream, on the east shore. Two men operated it, but whether they had been killed or had fled was unknown. There was wood waiting, but no sign of the choppers.

The Indians were on the other shore, farther upstream, but some might be in ambush, waiting for an attempt to get the wood. But with crews from three boats, and passengers from the *Pride of Kansas* for guards, the risk was not great.

A picked party went ashore, well armed, and proceeded to the deserted camp. Rawls was one of them, Whirter in command. Dudley and Earnshaw remained with the packets.

They found a man at the edge of the wood lot, as though he had been surprised at work. He had been dead for several days. There was no sign of his companion, no other reminder of trouble. Low hills rose back from the river, and a considerable growth of trees had been handy. Approximately half of these had been cleared.

"Poor devil!" McQuestion murmured, looking down at the dead man. "They made some money for a while, but he paid for what he got! I wonder what happened to his pardner?"

No one had an answer. While the others busied themselves loading the carts, McQuestion wandered about. There wasn't much danger, since watchers had been posted to keep sharp lookout.

To Rawls it seemed that McQuestion was moving with a goal behind his apparent aimlessness. Gradually he approached the patch of still uncut woods, then disappeared. Which might be a foolhardy thing, or a calculated risk.

Two could play that game. Rawls managed to

slip away from those whose business it was to keep
an eye on him. The woods were gloomy. Voices,
low but intent, came from a small, brushy coulee.
One was McQuestion's.

"It's agreed, then," McQuestion was saying.
"You let the first two boats get past safely. But you
sink the third—and take whatever you find on
it."

"And we get guns, whiskey!"

"You get guns and whiskey, once we're safely
past with the first two boats," McQuestion promised. "We'll put them ashore a couple of miles
up."

Presently McQuestion wandered back to join
the others, reporting regretfully that he had
found no sign of the second man who had worked
here.

"Mebby the poor devil got away and is still
wearin' his own hair," he added piously. "We'll
hope so."

Rawls was thinking hard. It wasn't likely that
McQuestion and Whirter had planned originally
to do any business with this war party, but they
were not above dealing with them when necessity
demanded—or betraying others to save their
own skin. The time spent since the *Pride* had been
fired on had given them the chance to get in

communication with the enemy. A few guns and a cask of whiskey would be a cheap price to pay for immunity for the *Varina* and the *Astrid*.

Such a bribe alone would not have been enough, with some renegade who knew his ability to sink the boats as they struggled through the Devil's Spin. But with one boat promised as a victim, and many passengers on board to yield scalps, a deal had been made. Whether or not it would be honored was another question.

This was a cold-blooded business, scarcely surprising in view of what McQuestion had already planned. Dudley was to be double-crossed. Indians would swarm out from both shores in canoes as soon as the *Pride* was crippled. It was unlikely that a single man would live to tell the tale. If any did, no taint would attach to the boats ahead.

This program couldn't be allowed to proceed. But the proper course of action was not so simple. Rawls might go to Captain Dudley and tell him what impended. If he did, Dudley was sufficiently hot-tempered that he'd demand a showdown then and there. That would pit Rawls' word against McQuestion's, and the latter would of course deny the whole thing. Whirter and Earnshaw would back McQuestion, bringing to light his own downriver record, the cloud on his reputation.

As a last resort, Rawls decided, he'd tell Dudley the facts, but only as a last desperate chance. The outcome was so one-sided as to be almost a foregone conclusion.

Already his mind was busy with another possibility. It was a risky course, but no more so than the other. If he could work it right, the *Pride of Kansas* should be as safe as the other river craft. As the wood was being loaded on board, he studied all three boats, noting their positions, cataloguing the chances.

He glimpsed Astrid, leaning pensively over the rail on board the boat of her own name, and though she made a pretty picture, he found himself unstirred by sight of her. His pulse no longer raced like a paddle wheel out of water, and the sense of pain had pretty well vanished along with the hopes he once had cherished. Part of that, he supposed, was due to discovering her duplicity, to the sureness that, however angelic she might at times appear, she was the daughter of her father.

But a part of his healing came from the presence during these weeks of Kathleen Garrison. She had shown a steady courage in the face of adversity which had compelled his attention, and they were partners in disaster. If there were shallows in Astrid, there were deeps in Kathleen.

Thought of her now was torment. However his coup came out tonight, his part would become manifest, and Dudley, once past the blockade, would no longer be around to befriend him, in turn, or to act as a deterrent upon the others. But that was a bridge to be crossed when reached.

"Pardon me, Captain, but shouldn't you be dressing?"

Earnshaw had come up and was watching with an amused glint in his eye. The man might be a villain, but he was capable of appreciating the sardonic humor of a situation.

"Dressing?" Rawls glanced down at himself. "I wasn't aware that I'd left off any indispensable garments."

"I refer to the dinner to be held aboard the *Astrid*. All the captains are being entertained by Mr. McQuestion. Miss Garrison, as owner, will accompany you."

Rawls recovered quickly. Here was more sardonic playfulness on the part of McQuestion. Astrid would be there, and Whirter, as captain of the *Astrid*. It was a situation calculated to put him in unpleasantly hot water, but that part didn't worry him now. The real trouble was that the dinner would take a lot of time, just when he needed it for something else.

Since there was no choice, he attired himself in his best uniform, and was presently joined by Kathleen and Narcissus. A touch of excited color had put roses in Kathleen's cheeks, and her eyes were sparkling.

"This should be interesting, at least," she breathed.

Rawls understood her perfectly, and nodded. "I'm not worried about it," he said. "Not with you along."

A dimple whose presence he'd never suspected peeped at him from her cheek. "That," she confided, "is the nicest thing you've ever said to me!"

"If the opportunity ever arises, I'll not be remiss that way," he promised, and felt the slight tremor of her fingers as they rested lightly on his arm. But he was filled with a heady sense of exhilaration. If Astrid anticipated a triumph, or Mark Whirter thought to watch him squirm, they were in for a disappointment.

They were welcomed aboard with considerable ceremony, though Astrid's face showed pale despite the excitement. She murmured a greeting, and that was all. Captain Dudley arrived, escorting a woman from his own boat—the only other white woman on any of the three. She was a passenger for Fort Benton, going there to join her husband, a Mrs. John Eller.

The meal was excellent and leisurely, the atmosphere gay, with an occasional false note. No one could legitimately know what the night might bring, or how the hazard of running the blockade might turn out. But it was kept in the background until the close of the meal. Then McQuestion brought it into the open.

"I've one suggestion before we go our separate ways," he said. "One reason why this party was held, with all women on board, is that, in tonight's little game, the *Astrid,* coming second, should have the best chance, everything considered. So I think it might be well if the ladies would remain on board here tonight—to perhaps comfort one another, and for such security as may be possible. Once safely past, each can return to her own quarters."

It sounded reasonable, the way he put it. Rawls heard the suggestion uneasily, along with the ready acceptance. *Damn the man!* he swore softly to himself, and shot a quick glance at McQuestion, ranged on to Mark Whirter. Did they have any inkling of what he had in mind? But that was impossible, since he had confided in no one.

Probably it was just a precaution on McQuestion's part, to have things under tighter control for the night. But it was decidedly upsetting to Rawls and his own plan. Though McQuestion didn't guess, the *Astrid* was slated to go third in line tonight, to be the boat which would feel the impact of renegade cannon.

Chapter Five

Rawls pondered uneasily as he returned to the *Varina*. The dinner had dragged long past the time which might reasonably have been required, as though the plotters were deliberately sopping up every moment until the time for action. If he was to carry out his own plan, it must be done without delay. And despite these new complications, still it must be done. There were a dozen innocent people on board the *Pride of Kansas* for every one aboard the *Astrid*.

The *Varina* and the *Pride* had tied up to trees along the shore, with lookouts posted to guard against possible surprise. But the *Astrid* had dropped anchor in the sluggish backwater, though she too lay close to shore.

Securing a coil of rope, Rawls kicked off his boots, divested himself of shirt and pants, then let himself over the side and down into the water as smoothly as a seal. It was cold, but he didn't

mind. Keeping in the deeper shadows of the
shore, he reached the *Astrid,* where the anchor
rope plunged tautly into the water.

Tying his own rope to it was simple. The next
part was tricky, to dive and swim under the
Astrid, coming up on the far side, near the shore.
There was always the risk of finding a pile of debris on the bottom, anywhere in this river, the
chance of becoming entangled in such a cluster.

But he reached the far side without incident,
climbed the bank and tied the other end of his
rope to a tree, pulling it tight. When the moment came to raise the *Astrid's* anchor, they
would have trouble, causing a long-enough delay to alter the plan.

One detail remained. He swam across to the
Pride of Kansas, and climbed on board without
incident, then moved soundlessly with bare feet.
He halted at sight of a shadowy figure. The outline was familiar, and he whispered Dudley's
name.

Dudley spun about, but he was a man of cool
nerves. His reply, though amazed, was guarded:
"Rawls! What are you doing here?"

"Testing out how good a watch is kept," Rawls
said lightly. "If I'd been an Indian, I could have
knifed your lookout and no one the wiser. But

we're getting out of here, and the point is this: The *Astrid* will be delayed in following, when I lead out with the *Varina*. Be on watch and swing in, right behind me. We'll let the *Astrid* go third tonight."

Dudley hesitated, perplexed. This was not according to agreement, and something was afoot. "Could you tell me why?" he asked.

"I could, but I'd prefer not to. I'm hoping you'll take my word that it's for your own good, and that of your ship."

He could almost see the workings of Dudley's mind. The *Astrid* carried Lomax McQuestion, and his reputation on the river was scarcely savory. Thought of the trickery associated with it ran in Dudley's mind. After a moment, he nodded.

"If you say so, all right," he agreed.

They gripped hands, then Rawls let himself back over the side. He reached the *Varina* and donned his clothes, with no one the wiser. It was still minutes early, but he gave the order to get under way. For the present he was in command, and men's lives hung on his decision.

Worse still, women's lives were involved, and that was a sharp thorn of worry in his mind. If the *Astrid* and those on board should fall prey to the grim horde who waited on shore . . .

But it was too late for a change of plan. Steam had been kept at the ready in the boilers, and the *Varina,* moving without a light, glided softly out of the backwater, the paddle wheel churning as they headed into the current. As Rawls swung out and past, the *Pride of Kansas* fell in behind like one duck following the lead of another. There was confusion aboard the *Astrid,* where frantic if silent efforts were being made to clear the obstruction and raise the anchor.

So far, all was going well. The *Astrid* wouldn't be long delayed, but now the position of the three packets could not be changed in running the gauntlet. The thin moon was gone, but the sky was clear of clouds, the stars giving sufficient light to outline the dark shores. A boat on the water was only a darker shadow, but it was hopeless to expect that the hawk-eyed watchers on the bank would fail to see them, particularly as they came under the muzzle of the cannon.

This was a run with a myriad of risks, not the least being what the Indians might do. Rawls had no sure way of knowing, but he suspected these warriors to be Sioux, led by a renegade, white or half-white—the man who worked the cannon.

An Indian's promise, once given, could be counted on. But a renegade's word was a leaky sieve, the balancing equation of honor left out. A lot depended on the councils which would have been held since that talk with McQuestion at the wood lot. They might well have decided that it would be foolish to have only a taste of whiskey from two boats, when the loot of all three was there for the taking.

Here the river ran ugly. At the far headwaters of a score of feeder streams the deep drifts of winter were in the last stages of disintegration, their dissolution being hastened by heavy rains. Consequently, the Missouri was high, and, channeled between rising rocky banks, a giant in fetters, the river roared in frenzy and bucked like an untamed cayuse.

Already the churning paddle wheels and the throb of the engines were smothered in the angrier pulse of the torrent. Sound would give no warning of their coming. The shores seemed to push toward them on either side, like the closing of a mighty hand. It was an illusion that Rawls had observed on other occasions, but twice as realistic and fearsome in the uncertain light. Now the engines on all three boats were straining to deliver full power, the progress of the fleet slowed to a crawl. There could be no burst of speed to sweep them past the danger point.

Earnshaw came up, ready to lend a hand in case of need. He shouted into Rawls' ear:

"Something's amiss. The *Pride* is second in line, the *Astrid* behind her."

"Nothing we can do now," Rawls retorted, which was the literal truth. He was calling on instinct to aid his faculties, since half a good riverman's skill is so derived. Normally a pilot could depend on his ears, the nuances of sound assuring deep smooth waters or warning of hidden shoals or rock, noises meaningless to untrained ears. But in the frothing turbulence of the channel they were entering, all sound was poured together into solid deafening thunder.

Now they were entering the Devil's Spin, one of the most dreaded stretches of water on the entire river. Bad enough by the full light of day, it was a churning inferno now, so that the packet vibrated to the straining engine and the *Varina* seemed scarcely to move.

They were riding the angry crest of the current, a delicate straddle which must be maintained. To slip off to either side would mean disaster. Once caught in the swirls and deep undertows, the hurtling power of tricky currents, even a river boat could be twisted and slammed against the rocky walls before the thrashing paddle wheel could get a grip and steady them.

The *Varina* was edging past the worst, but now they were coming to that stretch under the nose of the cannon. The river was widening again, the banks not quite so high. Scanning the west shore, Rawls picked out the spot where the cannon was likely to be hidden. That was where he'd place it if he was in charge, the best location available. This time he had to play a hunch, for if he was mistaken, it was the last error he'd ever make. There would be no chance to rectify it.

Twisting the wheel, he swung the *Varina* sharply closer to the shore. This was tricky business, coming in so close. A slight miscalculation could smash them on the rocky cliff.

"Take the wheel," he ordered Earnshaw. "Hold steady!"

Before Earnshaw understood what he had in mind, Rawls raced to the edge of the deck, poised, and leaped. For that one moment deck and shore were almost on a level. A gap of a dozen feet intervened, seemed to widen as the *Varina* suddenly started to sheer away. Then he was falling, clawing at the bank, legs and body dangling while his fingers grasped a scraggly bush and clung.

Drawing himself up, he started to run. Here

was sharply broken terrain where the elements had played rough games across the ages. But just above, not far back from the shore, he caught the sheen of firelight on a long strip of metal—the cannon.

What he could do, or how, was not clear in his mind, but on one thing he was determined. He had to put the big gun out of action before the *Astrid* came along. Tonight, McQuestion and Whirter shouldn't pay the proper price for their treachery. They must be given a fresh lease on life because of the others aboard the *Astrid*.

A tangle of brush was in his way, and he scrambled around it. Ahead was the cannon. And ahead also, crouching and alert, not quite sure what was going on but with suspicions aroused, was an Indian, tomahawk clutched in his hand.

Rawls scarcely slowed. Speed was essential here, speed and surprise. Apparently the Indian hadn't actually seen him jump from ship to shore, or it had been a shadowy leap that left him doubting whether or not his eyes were playing him tricks.

The warrior's back was half-turned. He spun as Rawls reached him, a fraction too late. The captain's big hands closed, twisting, the impetus of his rush in the grasp. It twisted the brave aside, hurled him over the brink of a twenty-foot declivity. But, as he went, Rawls' grasp on his arm shook the tomahawk loose.

Half a dozen men were huddled about the cannon, a gun crew outlandish by any army standards but trained for the job. At least four of them were Indians. The others might be whites or breeds; in their dress there was a scant difference which to the experienced eyes of Rawls branded them as renegades. Their attention had been caught by the brief turbulence of the struggle, but they were not sure what was happening.

He landed among them in a long jump, the tomahawk swinging. Rawls had a momentary glimpse of a painted face that had gone pale beneath the daub, and then the face was gone, almost decapitated by the swing of the axe. The others were falling back, not certain that this was a creature of flesh that had appeared so suddenly among them, momentary unreasoning terror driving.

That was the chance for which Rawls had hoped. The cannon was big, heavy, but it was set almost at the edge of the sharp declivity at the side. He bent and lifted, straining, and though his muscles cracked with the effort, something had to give. Abruptly it was toppling, crashing down upon the rocks below.

That had taken only seconds, but it was long enough for the others to recover from their flash of panic, to start back with yowls of rage and vengeance. Rawls ran, and now his old limp had returned to hinder him.

A gun discharged, the crack of it muted by the other noise, as was the wild yelling of a full score of painted warriors who had crouched and watched and waited for their moment. Realization that they had been cheated did nothing to improve their tempers. All of them were determined to take out their spleen on him.

He twisted and spun, and their numbers were against them, men getting in each other's way, hampering themselves. Two men were ahead, but twice as many were close behind. He threw the tomahawk, and now only one was in the way. There was a stink of renegade about him, and he had a revolver, an early model Colt's by the long-barreled look of it, and this he discharged full in Rawls' face—and missed. Before he could fire again, Rawls hit him, a blow that flattened and bloodied the beak of a nose and cleared the path.

The river was ahead, and Rawls poised for the leap, new strength surging into him at an unlooked-for stroke of luck. Like the *Varina*, the *Pride of Kansas* had swung in close to shore, accepting what he, as pilot, had chosen for the best channel. By now it was past, but the *Astrid*, third in line and close at the heels of the others, was following the same course.

Rawls landed on the deck of the *Astrid* and teetered wildly, while a tomahawk thudded into the planking beside him, amid a rain of arrows and a few rifle shots. Guns replied sharply from both the *Astrid* and the *Pride of Kansas*, and with the lessening pull of the current, all three boats were picking up speed.

Everyone was crowding around Rawls, exclaiming as they began to understand what he had done. Lomax McQuestion pumped his hand and found his own palm crimson, but he disregarded that and thumped him on the back with a heartiness that gave no indication of displeasure. Even Mark Whirter grudgingly complimented him on his exploit.

"It was foolhardy—but wonderful!" Kathleen said.

Astrid McQuestion was more eloquent. "You saved the lives of every one of us," she declared.

"And I'm as grateful—as deeply grateful, Denny
—as I've been completely a fool!"

It was almost as uncomfortable a moment as
when the Indians had seemed to have him surrounded. Reading the look in Astrid's eyes, he
knew that he had only to say the word to go on
from where they had been before—and that this
time she meant it. But somewhere in the running of the river, all the savor had been washed
from that salt.

All three boats halted for the remainder of the
night, a few miles upstream. Captain Dudley
looked sharply at Rawls as they came to a general
meeting the next morning, but he made no refer-
ence to the delay of the *Astrid* or to his own boat
going second, save to explain to McQuestion that,
when the *Astrid* had loitered, he'd figured it best
to swing in without waste of time.

McQuestion was not ill-pleased with the way
matters had worked out. If he had any suspicion
that Rawls could have guessed at what was in the
wind, it was not a thought to be voiced. And since
all three packets had made the run in safety, without the need to give any bribe, he could afford
to join in the general chorus of praise.

The *Pride of Kansas* was the first to take off,
Dudley waving and promising to see them again

at Fort Benton. There was delay for the other boats in getting under way—for a reason of which Rawls knew nothing at the moment.

Astrid, following a custom begun when she was first able to talk, and continued virtually without interruption since, was in her father's cabin laying down the law to her indulgent parent.

"I want Denny Rawls brought on board the *Astrid* for the rest of the journey!" she said, and regarded Mark Whirter coldly. "I made a bad mistake, back at St. Louis, listening to *him!*" she informed her father. "So did you! But it's not too late to rectify it."

"What do you mean, a bad mistake?" Whirter interrupted. "You're not putting that interfering Yankee ahead of me, are you, Astrid?"

"My understanding was that Yankees came from down East, around New England," she retorted, with a toss of her head. "Captain Rawls never saw New England in his life."

"That's quibbling," Whirter growled. "He's on the Yankee side, which is what counts."

"I thought I was doing the right thing when I helped you in that plot. It has succeeded, and what you do now doesn't concern me in the least.

But I've found that I made a mistake. It's Denny that I love, and that's all that interests me."

Her forthright declaration was no great surprise to Whirter. He had seen signs of it for some time, and only a few days earlier she had informed him bluntly that she cared for none of his love-making.

There was a stirring of jealousy in him, for it rankled to be displaced by another man. But he didn't greatly care. Whether Astrid or anyone else realized it, a moment of destiny was approaching—destiny for nations as well as individuals. In such a situation, lesser emotions didn't matter, nor did it count for much from now on whether or not he was slated to be son-in-law to Lomax McQuestion. Downriver that had been important and generally understood between the three of them—important not on account of Astrid, but because it gave him a needed leverage over McQuestion, who owned this boat.

That reason had pretty well vanished, as they'd discover one of these days.

"Do you think that Rawls is a tame puppy, to be whistled back to heel whenever you feel like it?" he demanded. "If you do, you're in for a surprise."

"No, I don't think that," Astrid confessed. "He's a man—which I'm only belatedly discovering." The unvoiced comparison brought a flush to Whirter's cheek, but disregarding him, she swung back to her father.

"I made a mistake," she repeated. "Now I want to correct it. So will you have him brought on board the *Astrid?*"

McQuestion shook his head. "No," he said. "And I'll tell you why. In the first place, that wouldn't help you. It would be too obvious. And in the second, he's needed on the *Varina*. You'll have a chance to see him, for both boats will stay together from now on."

He spoke boldly, hiding a cover of uneasiness, but to his surprise she raised no objection.

"Very well," she agreed. "In that case, I'll transfer to the *Varina*. It will be better for the womenfolks to be together. That's logical."

McQuestion looked at Whirter, and threw up his hands. "You see?"

Whirter shrugged. "You'll be placing the poor devil in hot water," he said. "That's all right with me."

Rawls witnessed the move uneasily. It was plain enough that Astrid had changed her mind, and she was not one to hide her emotions from the world. Many people appeared to have re-evaluated him during the course of the night. To his surprise, Sol Sherwood took occasion to speak as opportunity offered. He still walked like a pouter pigeon, but there was a new respect in his manner.

"You'd ought to be on our side, Cap'n," he said earnestly. "With what's comin', you're just the man we need."

"Just what do you mean by that?" Rawls asked.

Sherwood glanced around, then went on hastily. "You'll be findin' out what's in the wind," he confided. "All I can say now is, it's big. But since you're in it, anyway, one way or the other, wouldn't it be better all around for you to be in with us and get your share of the pickings? I can tell you this, Cap'n. After last night, all the boys would feel a lot better if you was leadin' us. You take over when the time comes, and we'll follow you to hell and back."

Winking, he turned and went about his business, leaving Rawls to ponder his meaning, and to wonder anew exactly what Mark Whirter had in mind. A while ago he'd figured it as merely a job of running whiskey and guns, but his suspicion was growing that it was bigger than that.

The inspection at Fort Pierre was only a formality. The *Pride of Kansas* had been making good time and had passed there the day before. Captain Dudley had recounted what had happened and spoken in glowing terms of the part played by Rawls. His presence was enough to satisfy the authorities that all was as it should be.

Which was an ironic compliment. Rawls would have preferred to have both cargoes confiscated, for that would put a period to contemplated mischief. But with Kathleen a hostage for his own conduct, he dared not denounce the others. Better to wait for another opportunity. It was a long way to Fort Benton.

He anticipated a rigorous inspection when Fort Union was reached, near the mouth of the Yellowstone. That was not only orders, but it was the beginning of the really dangerous country, where contraband cargo was concerned. But as they neared the border between Dakota and Montana territories, the *Astrid* dropped behind, so that only one boat would be visible at a time. McQuestion came aboard the *Varina,* and gave instructions to wait, then to proceed by night. Rawls eyed him in amazement.

"Do you aim to try to run past the fort in the dark?" he asked. "They'll be on the lookout for such a trick—they'll know that we're coming. It's risky business. In fact, I'd say it was virtually impossible. The Missouri narrows just above its junction with the Yellowstone, which gives mighty little leeway for slipping past."

"Never mind," McQuestion grunted. "Do as I say, and we'll see."

He volunteered nothing more until the broad push of the Yellowstone sent its beat against the Missouri, seeming to be the larger stream at this point. Then he gave his order.

"Swing up the Yellowstone. This is as far as we follow the Missouri."

Chapter Six

Rawls was startled. The Yellowstone was a forbidden river in a hostile land, reserved half by treaty and half by unwritten law to the Indians, taboo to white men. Swinging south and west, it was a broad watercourse draining a vast country. Such streams as the Powder, the Tongue, and the Big Horn flowed to join it. And here, ironically enough, it was the turgid tide of the Yellowstone that changed the Missouri from a clear, sparkling stream to a yellowish flood, altering it to the Big Muddy.

"You're familiar with the Yellowstone, aren't you?" McQuestion prodded.

"I've traveled it to some extent," Rawls conceded. "Though as to saying that I know it, that's something else. I suppose you realize that you're taking your life in your hands—the lives of everyone—in making a venture like this?"

McQuestion shrugged. "Any job that's apt to

pay big money is a risk," he said. "That's never stopped me yet."

"I don't mind it being your funeral," Rawls said drily, "but there are others to think of."

He was not alone in his pessimism. Astrid was gay, these days, coolly rebuffing Whirter, seeking anew to win the favor of Denny. To that end, she tried also to win the confidence of Narcissus, who had taken a real liking to Rawls. Her approach was oblique.

"I understand that you can read the future in tea leaves, Narcissus," Astrid murmured. "I've always been interested in anything like that. Would you read my future for me?"

Narcissus regarded her disapprovingly, turning from the unfriendly shores to a survey of the *Astrid*, its bow cleaving the water not far astern, paddle wheel making a froth where it passed.

"Tea ain' no laughin' matter," she told Astrid. "You mebby not like what it show."

"I'm sure I would," Astrid insisted. "Won't you try it, please?"

"All I do is read the tea," Narcissus warned. "What it tell not my business."

She made her preparations, while Astrid watched eagerly, but with a growing feeling of apprehension which she could not down. The clear amber liquid looked harmless, the leaves in the bottom of the cup no different from others which she had seen on numerous occasions. But as Narcissus drank the tea and stared somberly into the depths, Astrid realized suddenly that this was an alien and unfriendly land. It was as though giant forces had been set in motion which, like the river, could neither be checked nor controlled.

Narcissus' face was withdrawn, blank. Her voice came detached and sepulchral.

"Trouble," she intoned. "Trouble in the cup. Full up and spillin' over. You sowin' plenty trouble long way back. Now them seeds a-sproutin'."

Astrid strove to see, to have a look in the cup. It fell with a crash, splintering, a tiny dark stain spreading on the deck. Narcissus said not a word, but her eyes were burning. The angrily defiant words died unspoken on Astrid's tongue. Turning, she stumbled away.

It was easy to remind herself that tea leaves were only superstition, that she was Astrid McQuestion who had always gotten what she wanted, and that her father would continue to indulge her whims. She had made a misstep back in St. Louis —but she had realized it and wanted only to rectify it. Denny Rawls had loved her then. She had been desirable in his eyes, and she was unchanged now. She'd show Narcissus that tea leaves meant nothing. The thing to do was put an end to doubt and hesitation by going to Denny and getting this straightened out. That would make everything all right, and she'd lose no more time.

But Rawls was not in the pilothouse. The long-faced Taber was at the wheel, with the *Varina* barely creeping against the current, as uncertain in the bright sunshine as though it had been midnight.

"Cap'n Rawls is sick," he replied to her query. "He tried to steer, but he was pale as a rag and near as limp. And sweatin'. Sweatin' and shakin' at the same time." He shook his head. "I don't like it. We'll be in trouble if anything happens to him. Ever see a dirtier stream? You can't make out what it hides, no more'n if we was sailin' on tar."

"If he's sick, I'll go see him," Astrid said quickly. "He may need something."

Earnshaw was coming up, and he stopped her. "He's asleep now. I hope he feels better when he wakes up. Better not disturb him." He took the wheel from Taber, scowled at the water, and looked back at her.

"I don't like this," he said bluntly. "I don't

suppose Rawls knows much more what's down under here than the rest of us, but he seems to know by instinct where there's trouble. Somehow he keeps us going, though it must be a terrific strain. But Mr. Whirter insists that we keep moving, regardless. It's risky business without a pilot. Couldn't you talk to him?"

"Mr. Whirter? I'm afraid not," Astrid said coldly. "I have no influence over him."

From the way Earnshaw looked at her, she could almost read his thoughts. That she could exert influence if she tried; also that she owed it to the rest of them to subjugate her personal feelings to the good of the expedition. But she had no intention of making her peace again with Mark Whirter. It would have to be on his terms—that he become Lomax McQuestion's son-in-law.

That was all that he wanted, actually, or ever had desired her for. He'd worked through her to get McQuestion interested in this venture, the boats, the money and what it could buy. Nothing else counted with Mark Whirter. He was a cold, unfeeling machine, not a man. In his scheme of things, she was just another means to an end.

Wishing she might temper her refusal, she exclaimed suddenly and pointed: "What's that, Mr.

Earnshaw? Or who is it? Off there by the shore."

Earnshaw had already seen. It was a man, out just a few feet from the shrouding cottonwoods and dense undergrowth that made a green wall back from the river. The man waved his arms and appeared to be shouting, though the sound was drowned by the noise of the river and the engines.

He was a white man, but the incongruous part lay in his dress. A white man in this country must be a derelict or a fugitive, and in such a case one would expect to see him tattered and nondescript. This man was neither. He looked as though he might have strolled out from some big house on a fashionable avenue of an eastern city, instead of emerging from the wilds. He was carefully, even nattily, dressed, and somehow the sight of such a figure was twice as startling as a tattered fugitive would have been.

"Now what do you make of that?" Earnshaw demanded, his jaw slack.

"Shouldn't we find out?" Astrid asked practically.

Earnshaw twisted the wheel, then gave orders for a small boat to pick up the man on shore after approaching as close as was considered advisable. He was frankly puzzled.

"It could be a trick to lure us in for an attack," he said. "Though that hardly seems likely. But where would such a man come from?"

"If he was bait for Indians, he wouldn't be fixed up that way," Astrid answered his unspoken question. "We'll soon find out."

The fugitive stepped promptly into the boat as it approached, and was rowed back to the *Varina*. On board, he seemed no less odd. He was smooth-shaven, tanned almost to the color of saddle leather, so that, but for his bright blue eyes and clothes, he might almost have been mistaken for an Indian. That he was a dandified little man in speech as well as dress was at once apparent as he came forward, bowing sweepingly before Earnshaw and Astrid—but without removing his hat.

"A thousand thanks to you, sir, for this timely rescue, and a thousand pardons to both the lady and yourself for not doffing my hat," he exclaimed in a breath. "I, sir, am Schuyler DeMoss—a river pilot, sir, of whom you may doubtless have heard. Known somewhat widely as The Sky Pilot, not because of any proclivities on my part toward a dispensation of the Scriptures, but because I am a pilot and my name is Schuyler!"

He bobbed again, still without a pause for breath, and hurried on.

"The mystery of my presence, and of this somewhat incongruous attire, I shall attempt to make plain. I was pilot for the *Lady of the West*—a packet of which you undoubtedly know, sir. Her owner was Captain Prentiss—a well-meaning man, sir, but misguided. Having heard that there was unrest among the Indians, it was his hope that, by going among them, he might get at the root of the trouble; then, with gifts, of which we carried a more than ample supply, to placate them. A noble idea, but visionary. I doubted the efficacy of it—in point of fact, I spoke against it as foolhardy—but he was captain and I was hired to pilot the *Lady*. Which I did."

Mournfully he shook his head; then, still not leaving time for interruption, he continued.

"My knowledge of the Yellowstone is not great, though not entirely superficial. To hasten with my recital, sir, no misfortune was attendant upon the voyage itself. Disaster came when, seeking to make common cause with the Indians, we anchored too close to shore. Three days ago the *Lady of the West* was burned, looted, totally destroyed. I am, I fear, the sole survivor."

This time Earnshaw did get in a word. "Remarkable," he said.

"You refer, I know, to my attire." DeMoss sighed, and glanced disparagingly at himself. "A whimsy of fate, sir. I escaped from the *Lady* by diving overboard—in the natural, if the lady will pardon the expression. For hours I crouched low in the water near the shore, an unwilling witness to the orgies of the savages, and likewise a prey to mosquitoes where I even partially emerged from the water. My frame of mind, needless to say, was low. And then I had a stroke of good fortune. I came upon a box from the boat that had drifted with the current and lodged at an eddy.

"Captain Prentiss was a gentleman, sir, a well-meaning man. He had a more than ample wardrobe, and this was a part of it. Scarcely the garments for this country, I fear, but I was in no position to be choosy."

They listened in mingled interest and amazement, while the *Varina* lay at anchor. Those on board the *Astrid* had witnessed the rescue, and now she halted close by, and Lomax McQuestion, accompanied by Mark Whirter, came on board. DeMoss turned, eying them carefully, and again bowed deeply.

"Your pardon," he said. "And permit me to

explain the seeming discourtesy of remaining with covered head. I can only plead the excuse of vanity—an untimely emotion, I have no doubt. But I am bald as an egg, and I must confess to being sensitive. For that reason I have long made it a point to wear a hat at all times."

"Quite all right," McQuestion assured him, and listened with interest to a repetition of the story. Whirter was quick to seize upon the kernel.

"You say you're a pilot—that you took a boat up this river recently without mishap?"

"That is correct, sir," DeMoss agreed. "You will have heard of me, I expect—The Sky Pilot?"

"I'm afraid I haven't," Whirter denied. "But I'm a downriver man. Do you think you can pilot this boat until Captain Rawls recovers?"

"Why not?" DeMoss shrugged. "I must repeat the warning I gave Captain Prentiss, gentlemen —that this is an unhealthy country, and that I think you ill-advised to proceed upriver. But if you so decide, I at least have recent knowledge of the stream, which is at your service."

"Then let's get under way at once," Whirter instructed, and presently returned, with McQuestion, to the *Astrid*. Astrid herself was enchanted with the new pilot. That he knew his business was at once apparent, but he was com-

pletely new in her experience, a man with an in-
exhaustible fund of tales and, as he confessed, a
love for wagging his tongue.

"You're sure that talking to me doesn't distract
you?" Astrid asked belatedly.

"I must confess, ma'am, that you somewhat
take my breath away," DeMoss agreed readily.
"Not for a long time have I been in the presence
of your charming sex, and feminine beauty I always find heady as wine. But it's an experience
I would be loathe to dispense with."

Kathleen came up. She had been lying down,
had slept through the rescue and consequent
events, and now she was eagerly curious. DeMoss
was in his element.

"What a ship is this!" he said, and sighed
gustily. "Almost I shiver with apprehension. If
anything should happen to this expedition, such
a fate as overtook the *Lady of the West*—"

"Don't speak of such things," Astrid retorted,
and presently followed Kathleen to the hurricane
deck. "What do you think of him?" she demanded. "Isn't he right out of a book?"

"That's what I don't like," Kathleen said uneasily. "He seems to be. And somehow he doesn't
ring true."

"If you mean his clothes, he explained that,"

Astrid said, and told about them. "And he certainly seems to know his job as a pilot. I think he's wonderful."

Kathleen did not quarrel with her. Astrid had made an effort to be friendly, since coming on board the *Varina,* and though Kathleen understood only too well her real purpose, she had met her halfway. But it was a surface politeness. Even here, the only two white women in a vast reach of hostile wilderness, she could never be on intimate terms with Astrid McQuestion. There was too wide a gulf between them.

She hadn't known of Denny Rawls' illness when she lay down. Now that was an added worry. If anything should happen to Denny—

She checked the thought, realizing that it would be dangerous to follow it far. But if he was sick, she might be able to do something for him. And if he was well enough, he should know about this stranger from nowhere who, emerging from a wilderness, looked as if he had just stepped from a bandbox, and called himself The Sky Pilot.

Rawls answered her knock on his door, and sat sleepily up when she entered the cabin. He was pale and disheveled, but he protested that he was feeling better.

"Something upset me," he said. "I'll be all

right." He eyed her sharply. "Is something wrong, Kathleen?"

"I don't know," she confessed. "But I'm uneasy." She explained about DeMoss, and before she had finished, Rawls was on his feet, looking grim.

"Of course we could be mistaken, but I seem to detect an odor of rat here, too," he agreed. "Let's have a look at him."

Schuyler DeMoss's eyes narrowed as Rawls approached with Kathleen. Most of the day had run its course, a bright day of sun and cloudless skies, and now the sun was low in the west, long shadows reaching out from the cottonwoods along the shore. The country had changed during the hours while Rawls slept. The river valley was less broad here, the green wall of vegetation not so dense, allowing occasional glimpses of enticing meadows beyond.

But these were offset by the fantastic nature of the higher hills showing behind—rugged bluffs, weird and unbelievable, a succession of badlands which would endure for days as they progressed. Rawls studied them briefly, then turned his attention to the pilot. DeMoss, who had been unaccountably silent, bowed.

"Captain Rawls," he said, "this is a delight to which I long have looked forward, meeting the greatest riverman of them all. I trust that your indisposition is not serious?"

Rawls ignored the compliment and question alike, replying with a blunt question of his own. "So you're bald, eh?"

"Bald as an egg, Captain. As a peeled onion. And, though perhaps unjustifiably, vain—"

"That part I wouldn't doubt," Rawls grunted. With a quick gesture, he whipped the hat from DeMoss's head. Earnshaw frowned in surprise, and Astrid gasped at the indignity. It was exactly as The Sky Pilot had proclaimed—he had a completely hairless head.

But the removal of his hat seemed to have wrought a transformation in the man. For a moment he glared at Rawls, startled and uncertain, lips drawn back from snarling teeth, turned ugly in a second. Then, giving a violent twist to the wheel, he went into action.

It seemed as incongruous as for a rabbit to turn and fight, and somehow doubly terrible. From nowhere he produced a long-bladed, wicked-looking knife, and he sprang at Rawls with murderous intent. Astrid screamed, Rawls, unarmed, was in the path of a madman, moving too fast for anyone else to intervene.

It happened fast. Astrid closed her eyes to shut out the sight, but Kathleen watched closely, and yet she could scarcely follow it. Rawls did not step back or aside. But his foot shot out, the boot toe struck the pilot's knife arm and bounced it like a rubber ball held short in its jump by a string. The knife clattered on the deck, and Rawls leaped ahead.

Again the little man was like a rabbit, dodging nimbly. He evaded Rawls' clutching hands, reached the side and was off the boat in a leap, sending the water splashing high. In the same moment the *Varina* staggered to a jarring shock, throwing everyone on board off their feet.

By the time Rawls could regain his own footing, DeMoss, hairless head bobbing, was nearing the shore. A moment later he splashed through the shallows and vanished amid the undergrowth.

There was no time for him then. The engine was racing, the paddle wheel churning furiously, the *Varina* quivering like a creature that had received a mortal blow. Rawls shouted down the tube for full speed astern, and twisted at the wheel. But as he had expected, the reversed paddle wheel still beat helplessly. The *Varina* was hard aground.

"What the devil—" Earnshaw gasped, bewildered by the suddenness of what had happened. "Did *he* do that?"

"He aimed to wreck us, and no telling yet how close he's come to doing it," Rawls grunted. "Better take a look and see if there are any leaks. And arm everybody on board, fast, with plenty of ammunition!"

Earnshaw took a look at the inhospitable bank, now hardly a hundred feet away, and made haste to carry out the last part of the instructions. Rawls gazed about, revived somewhat by a freshening breeze across the water, one which swept away the mosquitoes that had begun to descend almost as soon as the packet came to a stop. He felt weak and sick from the day of illness, but there was no time to think of himself.

"But how did you know there was anything wrong with him?" Astrid demanded. "He was a white man, and he told a straight story. He fooled everyone else, even Father," she added thoughtfully. "And Mark Whirter. How did *you* know?"

"That he was a renegade? Three ways," Rawls explained. "First, his clothes. They could only have come from a looted boat or wagon train."

"But he explained that—"

"If they'd floated in a box in the river, they wouldn't have been in such fine shape. And then his lack of whiskers—"

"He was smooth-shaven," Kathleen nodded. "And that struck me as queer, that he would have had a chance to shave so closely."

"It would have been more than queer. But he wasn't smooth-shaven. He was hairless—with the whiskers pulled out by the roots, the same as the Indians do. That told me that he was a renegade who had turned Indian."

"I never thought of that," Earnshaw confessed sheepishly. "But the trouble started when you jerked his hat off. What did that mean?"

"I wanted to see his head, because he didn't want us to have a look at it. Part of it was hairless, all right—where the hairs had been pulled out —but there was a ridge where the scalp lock had been left. He'd done the best he could with that, shaving it close, and it would have fooled most people into the idea that he was bald. The trouble was that, even with a berry stain, it still showed pale compared to the tan on the rest of the top of his head—where, if he always wore a hat, the sun should never touch. When I pulled it off, he knew that the jig was up."

"Then he—he was sent to lure us to destruction!" Astrid felt weak. "But he—he seemed such a gentleman. He used such good English—"

"He hadn't forgotten that, which makes him useful as a stool pigeon," Rawls agreed grimly. "He's the worst sort of renegade—one who turns against his own people all the way, after having had all the advantages. Probably he had a record that would hang him if caught, so he had to go to the Indians. He liked that life, and went all the way."

Astrid shivered again, eying the darkening, unfriendly shores, remembering the glib phrases that had slipped off The Sky Pilot's tongue concerning female beauty. He had accomplished the first part of his plan to get them in trouble. And if the *Varina* met the same fate as he had ascribed to the *Lady of the West*—however fanciful a boat that might have been—then she would probably be taken alive, if possible. Recollection of Narcissus and her teacupful of trouble returned unpleasantly.

They had rounded a bend of the river only a few minutes before, and there was no sign of the *Astrid*, though it had been close behind them for most of the day. Kathleen scanned the horizon anxiously for smoke or other indication that it was close, wondering if some mishap had occurred. If they could work it, the Indians would like nothing better than to keep the two boats apart, unable to assist each other.

"There's no particular damage done, so far as I can discover," Earnshaw reported to Rawls. In this moment, Rawls was the captain, and everyone looked to him for guidance. Earnshaw's stomach felt queasy, and for the first time since leaving St. Louis, he had a twinge of doubt about this venture upon which he had embarked. It had sounded both feasible and profitable then, and there had been the added impetus of patriotism, with a chance to reap a handsome personal profit while doing great deeds for the South. But this was reality, and it was not at all the same. Now he and the others were forced to look to the man who had been betrayed, a man who was bitterly opposed to the entire scheme, or as much as he knew of it—but who was the only person who might save them now.

"Are we on sand or rock?" Rawls asked.

"Sand, so far as I can make out. But apparently we can't back off."

Rawls was already certain of that. They'd have to grasshopper again—if they could. It was too late to do anything more today. And daylight was a long way off.

Rifles from the supplies had been issued to all the men, and Rawls handed guns to each of the women.

"You look as if you had steady nerves and a good eye," he said to Kathleen. "You too, Astrid. And I'm sure that Narcissus won't hesitate to shoot an enemy. Comfort, you'd better get down lower, behind such barricades as we have."

"You think the Indians will attack?" Astrid quavered, the rifle feeling cold in her hands.

"They'll do more than try," Rawls assured her grimly. "The only question is how soon."

A wild chorus of yells gave answer. Rawls had hoped, not too strongly, that the Indians might wait for dawn, or at least for full dark. But they were losing no time. Perhaps a few minutes had been wasted in moving the watchful figures who had kept pace with them during the afternoon, skulking unseen just behind the green line of trees.

Now they had reached a point on shore and were ready. The sound was soul-shaking, as if coming from hundreds of throats, and then warriors burst from cover and started for them—

some in canoes, some wading out as far as possible, others going past that point and swimming recklessly, while a shower of arrows and a rain of bullets swept at the stranded *Varina*. Though she had carried contraband across a thousand miles, designed, as Rawls suspected, for some of these very Indians, even that wasn't working out as planned. Only one thing was certain. Death was swarming at them.

Chapter Seven

For the first time, Rawls was thankful for the guns, glad also that this was a hard-bitten, hand-picked crew who had come on this forbidden journey with the knowledge that they walked with danger. Survival now was measured in minutes, and the riflemen were wasting few bullets. Most of these men had undergone a baptism of fire in one army or the other, and they were steady now. They had need to be.

A wild figure was in the thick of the fight, directing the attack, exhorting the warriors to ever greater efforts. Schuyler DeMoss, hat discarded, coat flung aside, seemed the wildest savage of them all. He reached the *Varina* for a second time that day, set hand to climb aboard, and tumbled to the reddening waters beneath with his throat a gash where a bullet had torn. Earnshaw, crouching beside Rawls, nodded grimly.

"That pays back," he said.

Others, equally determined, were reaching

the *Varina* across a channel of death. Wild figures climbed, sprang aboard, to be met with bullets. But it couldn't last long, not at this rate. Too many were coming, determined to overwhelm the stranded packet in the first mad wave, to wash its decks in a wave of red. The somber shadows, the eerie rising hills beyond, were a fitting setting for day's end and journey's finish.

A sharper sound cut through the meleé, the angry blast of the *Astrid's* whistle. A ragged cheer went up from tortured throats as the *Astrid* churned toward them, a fresh volley from her decks cutting like hail among the attackers. Before that sweep, they wavered, broke, and scrambled frantically for cover.

None too soon. It had been a close thing, with boarders in hand-to-hand grip. Three men were dead on the *Varina,* five more wounded, two of them seriously. The shores were ominously silent as night rolled across the water, a blackness in which slinking figures could creep.

"It'll be an hour to moonrise," Rawls summed up grimly. "They'll aim to finish us before that."

"All we can do is fight them off," Lomax McQuestion rumbled. He had come across at the first lull in the fighting, his face strained and anxious. "We'll back you up. But lights would help them more than us."

"Most lights, yes," Rawls agreed. "But they'll swarm in the dark like ants over a crippled bird. There's just one way to stop them."

"What's that?" McQuestion demanded. "Name it and we'll do it."

"I'll have a try at it myself," Rawls retorted shortly. "You keep a sharp watch and hold them off."

It wasn't a job to be delegated, though the risk wasn't much worse than remaining on the boat for what was certain to come. That the Indians would take full use of this time of darkness, Rawls was virtually sure. Fever of battle was in their blood, the taste of victory had been on their tongues, and they'd savored it as a weasel lusts for hot blood. Rawls moved soundlessly over the side and into the water.

The river was cool, refreshing. His eyes were not too useful, for this first dark was like a blanket, the edges smotheringly drawn. The shadow of the cottonwoods, the darker loom of the uneven hills behind, crowded out the sky and mocked the light.

The water was lower than it had been a few

weeks before, flood crest for the season a month behind. Somewhere off here was what he sought, what he'd noticed briefly before the dark came down. He moved toward it, mostly by instinct, careful as he walked, though the ripple and gurgle of the water hid any splashing. There were rocks underfoot, moss-grown, slippery, and the current pushed strongly against his legs.

Something moved, a blacker shadow in the murk. These were waters in which men fished, their hooks the sharp weapons of war, their prey the stranded ones on the *Varina*. The warriors were moving back out to a fresh attack, and there would be just one way to fight them off—if he could manage it.

His feet came out of the water, and his hands told him what he wanted to know. Flood tide on the river had swirled here, across what was a small island during most months of the year. A tree, resisting the current, had stopped a lot of drift. It was piled high around the tree now, sticks nude to the sky and left to dry in the sun. A huge pile between boat and shore, though the bank itself rose with blacker intensity close at hand.

Rawls had brought some matches. He cradled them in his hands, finding small dry twigs by feel and building a tiny heap. The cupped flame hesitated, like a dog sniffing curiously at some new food. Then, finding it tasty, it gulped with huge appetite, the flame spreading fast. Rawls moved back into the river, away from the rising wave of light.

Cries tore the silence of the evening, a sudden hideous chorus of rage and alarm. But the tinder-dry driftwood was exploding into flame, the light spreading like the glow of a torch, revealing half a hundred figures who crept upon the *Varina*. Guns shouted hasty challenge, and Rawls, beside the boat, did not venture aboard until he had made himself known.

By the time he was back, the river was a second time deserted, cleared in panic quickness. Surprise had been cousin to terror while the flames leaped as if anxious to kiss the sky. Now the flames were subsiding, but the moonglow hovered like a night moth at the western edge of the badlands.

Lomax McQuestion was not stinting in praise. "You're the salvation of us all, Denny," he declared. "And that in return for the rotten mean way we treated you. Wurra, sad the day that I listened to the specious slickness of a tricky tongue! Were you but my son now, no man would be prouder!"

Astrid was approaching. Slender and graceful, in the reflected glow of the still-burning pile, she looked eminently desirable, and in that moment she was his for the taking, her lips framing a second to what her father had said.

"We've work to do," Rawls reminded them briskly. "There'll be a couple of hours more of black dark before the dawn, and no more wood for a flare. Either the *Varina* is off the bar before that or it'll never come afloat at all."

"You're the captain," McQuestion assured him. "But if she doesn't come off, everybody goes aboard the *Astrid*."

Kathleen stood in the background, watching. She, too, was framed by the firelight behind, her hair a halo in its glow. She'd handled a gun with the best of them when danger was a fingertip distant, and the *Varina* belonged to her. Half its cargo might be contraband, the crew in McQuestion's pay, the boat itself stranded in forbidden waters, but the *Varina* must float free.

"We'll have to grasshopper her off," Rawls added. "Everybody keep guns handy."

Earnshaw stared, incredulous. It was one thing to grasshopper a boat off a bar in daylight, and with no worse menace than the passing of time to hinder. To do so in a few scant hours of moonlight, when men's movements could be seen and guns and arrows twang out from the shore, was something else. But nobody voiced objection.

Grasshoppering was a fairly common practice on the Big Muddy. Like most boats that plied the river, both the *Varina* and the *Astrid* were equipped for it, with a pair of spars carried along to be used if the boat ran aground.

Under Rawls' direction, the spars were raised and set like posts in the river, one on either side, with the tops inclined toward the bow. Nothing happened while that was done. Apparently the Indians had not yet recovered from their double setback, or else there was no one familiar with the operation to warn them of what was happening.

But the lull ended as the rigging began. Above the line of the deck, each spar must be rigged with a tackle block, then manila cables passed over these, one end fastened to the gunwale, the other wound around the capstan. This entailed climbing, and the operation was in its middle when the man at work screamed and all but fell, an arrow quivering in his arm.

Rawls jumped and climbed, grabbing the half-tied rope before everything could crash in a tangle. The other man fell back, and now more arrows were coming, guns taking up the chatter. Rawls worked grimly, unheeding, until the job was done.

"And the devil of it is, we've no targets to shoot back at!" McQuestion fumed.

Rawls disregarded him. "All set," he said, and at his order the capstan turned, the paddle wheel revolved, and the *Varina* was lifted and pushed along. Not enough to free her, but Rawls hadn't expected that. The Sky Pilot had run them hard aground, and it would be a race against the encroaching dark as well as the hostiles on shore to get it off in time, with the process to be repeated over and over until they floated free.

It was not by chance that the process was called grasshoppering. When the spars were set, the boat bore a grotesque resemblance to a grasshopper, with great ungainly legs poised, and when it did move, it was in a series of hops.

Those on shore kept up a constant harassment, against which there was no defense. But beyond that first lucky shot with the arrow, the Indians scored few successes. The light was tricky, and the distance long for bows, while with guns they would take no prizes for marksmanship. But the strain on the nerves made the night drag even while it seemed to race.

Kathleen, watching like the rest, held her breath each time the *Varina* moved, felt the same ache of disappointment as it still held fast after the hop. There was unreality in this situation, the black sheen of the river with stars shivering in its mirror, the moon creeping above. Even the guns, the arrows, and the Indians were like a bad dream from which she must finally awake. Only the *Varina* and Denny Rawls held reality.

Across two thousand watery miles they had come to be her world. She'd liked the looks of Denny that night at The Planters, a man standing tall and cocksure, but without conscious arrogance—and despite all setbacks, he'd lived up to that reputation in the intervening weeks.

Her heart had cried out against the hurt in store for him, from which she had striven vainly to save him. If her motives had been half selfish, they were no longer so. She felt like crying out when he walked exposed and a gun spat at him, and her flesh cringed when she was sure that he was hit.

But this was a battle beyond the physical. More than ever it was a fight for control—of men and of things, of emotions and hearts. The values had changed and the stakes had shifted, but the struggle was becoming each day more intense. They'd win tonight, because Denny was the captain. But what of the days ahead?

From another part of the deck, crouching behind a shelter, Astrid watched with the same intensity. She'd been a fool, she realized bitterly. At long last, she knew what she wanted, and knew that it was out of reach. Once the cup had been at her lips and she'd cast it aside.

There lay the irony, for she had done it for Mark Whirter, and Whirter now was the big question mark of this whole mad adventure. Back at St. Louis he'd played the lover and deferred to her father. But the idea had been his, and what wild dream actuated him she was yet to learn. He'd told only a part of his plan, a part of the truth.

She sensed an unsuspected strength in him, a coldness of purpose that could be ruthless. He was a silent man, but behind the silence was a purpose bordering on fanaticism.

A shout went up, and as the moon went out of sight, the *Varina* was afloat again. Time to go to bed. Astrid groped, her eyes dry and hot. Morning or waking would bring no end to nightmare.

Lomax McQuestion returned aboard the *Astrid* with his mind made up and a bitter taste in his mouth. It was galling to his pride to concede that he had been a dupe, led on a wild adventure by clever words which had painted a dream of avarice, now a blown bubble in the wind. Increasingly he had come to distrust Mark Whirter, to sense, like Astrid, that the man was a fanatic. And fanatics, as McQuestion had long since learned, were uncertain pilots who steered by a strange compass.

Well, he'd been a fool, and this venture was a failure. Better to acknowledge his mistake, take his loss, and get out with a whole skin while he could. Danger had never bothered him, but there was Astrid and the other women to think about. He'd acquaint Whirter with his decision and have it over with.

That there would be trouble he knew. Like Astrid, he'd come to sense the strength in Mark, along with a growing stubbornness. But the man must realize by now that the whole scheme was mad.

Whirter had remained aboard the *Astrid,* anchored ready to lend a hand if the fight grew too hot. He, too, was a man unworried by danger or personal risk. That quality, along with a natural flair for leadership, had made him one of the youngest captains on the river. It had quickly gained him a captaincy in the Union army, where he had served only that he might spy and betray for the South, which he loved with a passionate devotion. For it, he would go to any length, insisting that the Cause came above all else.

He'd painted a glowing picture. Two boats on the Yellowstone, with guns and whiskey for the Sioux. Already they were on the warpath. Win their good will with liquor, inflame them to new high zeal, gain other adherents from other tribes, arm them for a flaming crusade across the wide border. It should reap a rich harvest of fur in return. The warriors could be counted on to pay more for guns and drink than for beads and blankets such as others offered.

It had sounded good, back at St. Louis. But the Indians were hostile to all whites, without regard for the thing in a man's mind, so the whole scheme was out of the question. Bluntly, his face haggard in the dawn light, McQuestion told Whirter so.

Whirter listened in silence. He could be impassive, a disconcerting quality against which the steel of anger blunted its edge. Now he asked a question.

"What do you propose to do?"

"We've no choice," McQuestion retorted. "You

wanted to go a lot farther before we tried making a deal with them, in hope of finding a friendlier tribe. That's out of the question now. We've got to turn back."

"And throw our cargo overboard for the fish?"

"The contraband, yes. We'll head back for Fort Union, then up to Benton with the rest. It's my money that is being lost. All you lose is the profit you hoped to make. But I'm damned if I'll put profit above the lives of Astrid and everyone else."

Whirter regarded him unblinkingly. "You're forgetting something," he said coldly. "Quite a few things, in fact. The *Varina* belongs to Miss Garrison, and we've been guilty of piracy and a few similar crimes. Holding by force. That applies to Rawls as well. They'd be in a position to send us to prison for long stretches—or, more likely, before a firing squad. Have you thought of those things?"

"I think they'll be reasonable," McQuestion grunted. "If they aren't, I still prefer that to the other."

"In other words, you figure that you can settle with them, and if the damn Yankees take me off your hands, it'll be good riddance. I'm to be the sacrificial goat. Well, I don't happen to see matters in the same light, McQuestion. That wouldn't appeal to me."

"I didn't say anything of the sort—"

"But you thought it. And I don't like it. This seems to be the time to place my cards on the table. Maybe you'll change your mind when you see them. We'll make a try at an alliance with these Indians. When they understand that we're on their side, and that the Union boys in blue are against them, they should be reasonable. We can use their friendship and cooperation as well as the fur. Also, they can make a lot of extra trouble for the Yanks after they're well armed. But that's only a small part of my scheme—the least important part."

McQuestion stared. "What the devil do you mean?"

Whirter's eyes glowed. The fanatic was coming to the fore.

"I'll tell you. You know how they've found gold at Virginia City, at Alder! Two of the richest gold strikes the world has ever known. From what I've heard, those camps are swarming with men who are taking out millions! More to the point, there's an organization in those towns, men who call themselves the Innocents! Some people would call them road agents, outlaws. As a matter of fact, they're patriots—secret agents of the Confederacy! I've been in touch with some of their leaders since last fall."

McQuestion eyed him in amazement. "I think you're crazy!" he said.

"Think what you please. I know what I'm doing. I've made the arrangements with them, long in advance of leaving St. Louis. When we get as far as we can go by boat, they'll meet us with horses for transportation overland. We'll make a quick trip, strike the gold camps without warning, and working with the Innocents, who are scattered everywhere, make a tremendous haul. Then back to the boats and downriver—all the way down to the Confederate lines with that gold! It will be a lifesaver to the Cause!"

"So that's it!" McQuestion was beginning to understand, and his disgust mounted. "You've led me on this wild-goose chase with the notion of getting gold for the secesh!"

Whirter's face flamed. "Careful what you say! I'm a Confederate, and I don't like that term! I thought you were a patriot, too."

"South or North, it's all one to me, as you've known all along," McQuestion growled. "Their quarrels make good pickings, and the devil take the hindmost! But let's be practical. The Confederacy is on its last legs. It's sure to lose."

"I don't agree with you. We need money, and this gold may be the difference between victory or defeat! It won't take much to tip the scales and secure allies—European nations that have favored us all along but have hesitated about declaring themselves openly! If England should declare war against the Union—"

"She won't," McQuestion contradicted him. "The English government rather leans toward the South, but the people over there favor the North, and their government knows it. And Russia is just looking for an excuse to strike at England if she becomes involved! Not that Russia cares anything about the United States, but she hasn't based fleets at San Francisco and New York just to admire the scenery!"

"But those fleets have finally moved out," Whirter said triumphantly. "I got that news a while back. They're making the same mistake as a lot of others, thinking the war is about over. That's the time to hit them, and that's what we're going to do!"

"Your scheme is too fantastic for any use," McQuestion repeated. "As to going overland to the gold camps, how could you get anywhere with the Indians hostile?"

"That's why we want to win them if we can," Whirter said. "Though even if they don't side with us, it doesn't matter too much. We've a picked crew of fighting men aboard both boats, all of them pledged to the Cause. There'll be a big escort from the Innocents to help us."

McQuestion chose not to argue that for the moment. He picked on another point. "What's that about the crew?" he asked sharply.

"Just what I say," Whirter retorted. "I picked them—every man on both boats, with the exception of Rawls. They know what this is about, and they'll go through with it."

Lomax McQuestion was breathing heavily.

"Of all the gall!" he spluttered. "I furnish the boat, I pay the bills—and all that I'm used for is a cat's-paw!"

Whirter shrugged. "Call it that if you like," he acknowledged. "It'll be simpler, with less trouble all around, if you understand the situation. But before you get all riled, let's get the facts straight. I promised you a good profit from this venture, and you'll get it. We'll get gold, lots of gold, in addition to fur. You get your share, exactly as I agreed with you at the start."

McQuestion became thoughtful, as Whirter had known that he would. Then he shook his head.

"It's too wild a notion," he said, almost regretfully. "I wish I could see any way of working it, Mark. It's the biggest, most beautiful scheme I've ever heard of, and I've run across some lallapaloozas in my day. To hold up a gold camp and get away with millions! Yes, it's a great scheme. But completely unworkable."

"We have a loyal crew back of us," Whirter argued. "The Innocents will guide and help when we get there. We'll have the element of surprise when we strike. It can't fail."

"I wouldn't trust these Innocents you speak of as far as I could swim behind the paddle wheel," McQuestion grunted. "You say they're outlaws. They'd be no good."

"They're called outlaws," Whirter said. "So are we. That's a blind. Actually they're patriots. They have a strong organization, with the whole community honeycombed and undermined. Why, even the sheriff is with us—he's the chief of the Innocents! I tell you, it can't fail!"

Unconvinced, McQuestion shook his head. "You've lost your judgment," he said. "But it might stand a chance if the Indians were for us.

If we can find a way to win them over, that would change the picture."

"That's what we've got to do," Whirter agreed. "When they understand, they're bound to be for us."

"There are white men among them," McQuestion said, thoughtful now. "That pilot proved that. We might try a flag of truce, let them know we want to be friends, that we have whiskey."

"Better get Rawls to help with that angle," Whirter suggested. "He knows the Indians of this country."

"I'm not too sure that he'll lend himself to such a job," McQuestion demurred.

"Leave that to me," Whirter said.

And, back aboard the *Varina,* he put it bluntly up to Rawls.

"We have guns and whiskey aboard, Rawls, as you've known all along, and you know why," he said. "We figure it would be better to bribe them to peace, if we can, and get out of here alive. Don't you agree?"

"The mood they're in, I doubt if they'll deal with us, but it's an idea," Rawls agreed. "Though even that's risky."

"We'll have to make a virtue of necessity," Whirter murmured, and pulled at his chin.

"We'll start out with a gift of liquor, to show our good will."

"I'm willing to try and buy that, with whiskey," Rawls admitted. "But I won't agree to giving them guns."

"I'd hesitate also about arming them," Whirter said. A first step was what counted. If that was successful, he'd be in a position to handle affairs his own way.

It was agreed to lower a boat, and to load whiskey into it with great ostentation, then to go ashore under a white flag. McQuestion shivered, but he could see no other choice. The first part of the operation was performed, sure that unseen eyes watched. Then they rowed toward the shore. Under the protective rifles of the crews, they halted some distance from the bank and McQuestion raised his voice.

"We bring whiskey," he said, hopeful that someone could understand. "Whiskey for a gift. We want to parley."

He waited while a minute passed, and the river and the shore seemed empty. Then a reply came back.

"Ugh. White man and Indian talk."

Even with that fundamental agreed upon, it took time. Time for the Indians to sample the contents of the keg and make sure that this was no hoax. A conference between leaders on both sides was agreed upon for the afternoon, a conference at which the white man could unburden himself and the red man would consider his words.

"And if they don't approve of our ideas, they can turn them down and have a new try at killing us," Rawls pointed out. "They don't have anything to lose. All we have to lose is our hair!"

"Meanwhile," Mark Whirter said piously, "it gives us time to consign our dead to the deeps of the river, with proper Christian ceremony."

Chapter Eight

McQuestion and Rawls went ashore, accompanied by several of the crew. McQuestion was confident now. If the Indians were willing to talk, matters would work out. Since he had gifts for them, it would be to their interest to accept.

Whirter remained aboard the *Astrid,* the crews keeping out of sight but with guns handy. Once ashore, Rawls was able to confirm his earlier opinion. These were Sioux, just as that war party at the Devil's Spin had been. He pointed this out to McQuestion.

"So long as they're willing to parley, what difference does it make?" McQuestion asked, and Rawls shrugged.

Red Cloud was chief of the Sioux, but apparently he was not in this vicinity. There were lesser chiefs present to do the talking. They listened gravely while McQuestion explained that they

came in a spirit of friendship, bringing firewater
for their allies. Rawls interpreted.

"Firewater is good," was the reply. "But we
need guns. How about rifles?"

Rawls relayed the question. "If you furnish
them guns, count me out," he added bluntly. But
McQuestion was given no opportunity to answer. A newcomer arrived, stalking up to join the
group, glaring at the white men. Angrily he ha-
rangued the others, and it appeared that this was
news which had just arrived, but it was full of a
grim import. Softly Rawls explained to McQuestion, seated beside him.

"He's telling them that an agreement was
made to give them one boat and all the loot on
board it, back at the Devil's Spin—and all the
scalps of those on that boat!"

Color drained away from McQuestion's florid
face, leaving it flaccid. He moistened suddenly
dry lips with his tongue, his eyes darting nerv-
ously.

"He says there was treachery there on the part
of the white men, men in boats such as these,"
Rawls added softly. And then he hissed a warning: "Sit still!"

But his own scalp was crawling in anticipation.
His impulse, like McQuestion's, was to make a

dash for the small boat waiting at the shore, but that wouldn't do. Yet to wait was to die, for now the messenger was coolly adding the damning details that it was McQuestion who had made that other agreement. The verdict had already gone against them.

The harangue was still going on, the messenger giving the grim details of how men had died at the Spin, because of some of these same white men. Taut with tension, the Indians still listened, but they were like bows strung and ready to loose. In their present mood they would repay what they counted as treachery with more of the same.

There was just one chance. The white men had come unarmed, McQuestion arguing that a show of friendliness and trust was essential. Rawls had had no choice but to obey orders.

One of the chiefs sat close at hand, and he had not been so foolish as to lay aside his weapons. He had a tomahawk in his girdle, and Rawls moved like a pouncing cat. He brandished the axe at its owner's eyes before the others were quite sure what was happening.

"We go back to boat," he grunted in English, using it for the sake of his companions. "Nothing happen to us, nothing happen to you. If we die, you die too!" Quickly he repeated it in

Sioux, so that there would be no misunderstanding.

McQuestion was staring, getting to his feet. He had been in plenty of tight places, but the turn which this had taken was the worst he'd ever been in. Watching the newcomer, he had belatedly recognized him as the man with whom he'd talked at the wood lot, making the deal that was to have destroyed the *Pride of Kansas* and sacrificed the lives of those aboard her.

Now Rawls knew of that treachery, but the fact that he would be a chief target for vengeance was uppermost in his mind. If he lived these next few moments, it would be due to Rawls! McQuestion gestured, and the crew members turned to move with him, Rawls at their rear, the tomahawk menacing the chief.

Momentarily it was working. The other chiefs watched, stunned, well aware of their comrade's peril at a false move. But an Indian didn't think like a white man, as Rawls was aware. The life of another man, a hostage, wouldn't weigh large with them, not for long.

Clouds were building in the west, taking dark shape above the twisted hills, and a cool breath blew down the river. Those on the packets were alert, guns trained on the Indians visible on shore.

But for every red man visible there was a score out of sight but within striking distance, and without turning his head as he walked, Rawls could sense the anger which ran through them, could almost catch the hot stench of it rising around him.

The small boat was only a few feet away when his hostage precipitated action, twisting about and hurling himself at Rawls, sinuous and deadly as a rattler in coil. Hell exploded as though he'd jarred loose the cap.

Rawls' swing with the tomahawk missed, and the Indian's grab slid along his arm and wrenched savagely for control of the weapon. It dropped between them, while rifles on the *Varina* and the *Astrid* began a quick, angry chatter. Men were swarming at Rawls, paint-bedaubed devils out of a nightmare. In their minds there was full justification, and he couldn't blame them. But the ethics of battle offer scant consolation to those who fight them.

He went down beneath a greasy swirl of bodies, but they were hampered by their own numbers and fury. Rawls twisted, rolled, and the river was at hand and friendly, its muddy tide pulling him away. He dived, swam, and came up close to the *Varina*. The round eye of a gun glared black at him, jerked up as Kathleen recognized who it was. The attack was still furious as he was helped aboard.

Presently it slackened, for thwarted anger was no match for the guns on the river boats. Even so, the toll had been heavy. Two men killed, three others hurt in that latest skirmish, and they had been unable to bring away their dead. Of the injured, Lomax McQuestion was worst off, his scalp laid open by the glancing blow of a war axe that had just failed of its objective. Bleeding badly, and as near dead as alive, he was hoisted aboard and bandaged up.

Mark Whirter had watched and directed the resistance with cold calculation, not particularly surprised or much disappointed. He'd long since written off the trading in his own mind. Now, with McQuestion unable to resist, he took command.

Whirter came across to the *Varina* in the dawn.

"We'll go on," he instructed. "Rawls, I want you to take both boats to that big rock that Lewis and Clark named Pomp's Pillar. We've wasted too much time here."

"Go on?" Rawls repeated, amazed. "What's the point in that? After what happened yesterday—"

"What happened yesterday doesn't make any

difference," Whirter said tightly. "I've had other plans in mind from the start of this trip. Nothing has occurred to alter them." He had explained those plans to McQuestion, but he saw no reason for giving details to Rawls, who would be bitterly opposed. "Your job is to pilot us, the same as before."

"That's easy to say," Rawls retorted. "Doing it is something else. We're not far from the mouth of the Powder. Other boats have found the Yellowstone navigable to that point. One or two, they tell me, have even reached the Big Horn, though that would be a touch and go proposition at any time, and particularly with the river dropping as fast as it is these days. Pomp's Pillar is some miles beyond the Big Horn. What you're asking is out of the question."

"Maybe," Whirter conceded. "But let's understand each other, Rawls. I'll take the risk of the boats. Your job is to pick a channel and get them along. I picked the crews for both boats, back at St. Louis. They're behind me, and that leaves you no choice in the matter. Do I make myself plain?"

Rawls shrugged. "I suppose you know what you're doing," he conceded. "Running farther and farther into hostile country. If we keep on, none of us will return."

"I'm not convinced of that. But if we don't, we'll have made a good try. Earnshaw, get the *Varina* under way. Rawls, you can pilot as you've been doing, or do the job in irons. It's up to you, and of no consequence to me."

Rawls was puzzled by what seemed an incomprehensible action. He was not the only one. Astrid came to the pilothouse as she felt the boat in motion; she could tell by the steady beat of the engine and the powerful thrust of the paddle wheel that they were again breasting the current, not starting back down the river.

"What's going on?" she demanded. She had just left her father's bedside, where McQuestion, usually so florid and hearty, lay in a half-stupor, looking pale and close to death.

"Whirter's orders," Rawls explained. "He says we're going to Pomp's Pillar. He didn't say why."

"Pomp's Pillar?" She was aghast. "Isn't that a long way farther upstream?"

"Something over two hundred miles, as I figure it. It may be closer to three."

"And you're taking the boat—taking us all to destruction?" She swung on Earnshaw as he appeared. "What's the meaning of this—this folly? My father owns the *Astrid*. I demand that both boats be turned back, at once."

"You'll have to talk to Mr. Whirter," Earnshaw retorted. "He's in command."

"Since when?" Astrid demanded hotly. "My father commands."

"You'd better talk to Mr. Whirter," was all that Earnshaw would say.

Astrid hesitated, then went back to see her father. McQuestion had recovered consciousness, though he was weak and feverish. It was no time to bother him, as she realized. On the other hand, his life, and the lives of all of them, might hinge on what was done now, and so she told him what was happening. McQuestion groaned.

"The man's a lunatic," he said. "But I'm afraid we're in his power." Grimly he explained what Whirter had told him of his real intentions. "He'll end up by getting us all killed," he prophesied. "But so long as the crew will follow him, I don't know what we can do."

"We'll do something," Astrid vowed. With clearer insight than some of the others, she understood that neither the hazard of hostile Indians nor anything else would swerve Whirter from his purpose. Getting the gold had been his real objective from the start, and he was enough of a fanatic to go through with it or die in the attempt. If the rest of them died with him, that was a small matter.

Briefly she considered. There were three courses open, and none of them sounded promising. But she must do something. She sought out Earnshaw again.

"I know now what is planned," she told him directly. "To make a raid on the gold camps. But under these conditions, that's the wildest sort of folly. Surely you can see that, Mr. Earnshaw?"

Earnshaw shook his head. "Whether I think so or not, I have no choice but to obey orders," he retorted. "It so happens that Mr. Whirter is my superior officer—a colonel in the Army of the Confederacy. I am a captain in the same service, and pledged to support him."

"And the crew are Confederate soldiers?"

"Some are. Others belong to the Confederate Navy."

Astrid bit her lip and turned away. She realized helplessly that Whirter had planned well, picking his men with care. In a hostile land their only salvation lay in sticking together, obeying their leader. Unless and until it was borne in upon them that they were going to their death, they would do as he said. Even if they came to realize the hopelessness of the situation, mutiny against such a man as Mark Whirter would not be easy.

So long as he had an unquenchable faith in his ability to carry through the plan he'd formed, he could transmit that same faith to the others. They had entered upon this venture with a full knowledge of the risks, as invaders of enemy territory. In a way it was breath-taking, magnificent. But men of that caliber had something of the same fanaticism as their leader, and would be hard to sway.

There were two remaining chances. For the second, she swallowed her remaining pride and sought out Denny Rawls, finding him, as she had hoped, alone in the pilothouse. Briefly she outlined what Whirter had in mind.

"You've got to help us, Denny," she pleaded. "I've been a fool, used and hoodwinked. But this is folly. Don't you agree?"

"It's folly," Rawls conceded, "but much as I dislike the man and his motives, I'll have to admit that it's magnificent folly. The same sort that Hannibal was guilty of when he decided to cross the Alps. I didn't know that Whirter was that big a man. I thought he was only after a quick, cheap profit, with no scruples as to how he got it."

Belatedly he realized how patly those words applied to Lomax McQuestion. Astrid colored, but her voice was steady.

"It's a terrible mess," she said. "You must hate and despise us all—me most of all. But you're the real leader here, Denny. The men all respect you, and they know that without you we'd have met disaster long before this. You must do something."

Her eyes said more than her lips, giving him a promise that he had only to ask to receive. Rawls looked away, and she colored, aware of the hot rush of shame to her face. Always in her pampered life she had had only to ask. No one had thought of refusing her. But when she'd trifled with this man, she'd lost him, and too late she was coming to realize what she had cast aside.

No need to plead with him. Whatever he thought of her or her father, they were allies in this, and he'd do what he could. But she knew that he would do it in his own way and in his own time. There were two strong men on this venture, and each, in his way, cast a long shadow. Power was concentrated in the hands of Mark Whirter, but the contest was less unequal than it might appear. So far as she was concerned, there remained a third chance—to have it out with Whirter.

Never before had she been afraid of any man, but now her legs were rubber.

Denny Rawls, limping slightly as he moved about the pilothouse, stared with absorption at the waters just ahead of the questing bow of the *Varina*, shifting his glance farther upriver, then to the shores and finally to the sky, gray and lowering today. The patch of cloud that had blackened the west the evening before had brought a mutter of thunder and a few light spatters of rain. But after that it had thickened and spread, and the day was in keeping with the prevailing mood aboard the two packets.

They were in for trouble. The engineer had complained both to him and to Earnshaw that the engines were getting in bad shape. A trip up the Missouri was no picnic for the men who nursed the engines, any more than it was a rest cure for the wood-hungry power plants. Two thousand miles they'd come, and the engines on both boats were showing the strain.

Rawls knew the procedure, common to every well-run river boat. Iron boilers were tricky things, with the ever-present threat of blowing up unless you nursed and pampered them along. The water of the Missouri, like that in the Yellowstone, carried a lot of mud. That mud must be blown out at frequent intervals by a tube properly adjusted in the boilers; otherwise, the life of any boiler proved short indeed, and with it, the life of ship and crew was equally brief.

They had come too far too fast; despite the best care they could bestow, the boilers were rusting.

And the engines were greedy for fuel. Soon they'd have to get more wood. Which meant cutting their own, harassed by hostiles.

Added up, the hazards were impressive, but Mark Whirter, an old hand on the river, knew them all without being told. That was what made Rawls admire the man in spite of himself. Foolhardy, crazy, call it what you would, it took a big man to envision such a scheme, or to have the courage to push relentlessly ahead.

"What's it all about, Denny? Why are we still going on?"

It was Kathleen who asked, and the old-timers said that it took a trip up the river to get to know a man—or a woman. If that was so, Kathleen was standing the test. Deeply concerned as she was, she accepted things as they came, not complaining.

"This is a trip to the moon," he said gravely, and told what he had learned of their real des-

tination. There were facts that couldn't be recon-
ciled, mental quirks and actions that didn't fit.
Up to now these had bothered Rawls' relentlessly
logical mind, but they did so no longer. For himself, he'd never reach the heights of imagination
to which Mark Whirter soared, but he could understand such a man.

Where there was a flash of genius there were
also gaps. Generally those turned out to be weak-
nesses to wreck a man before he attained his goal.
Few had the skill or the luck of a Hannibal.

"You mean," Kathleen asked, "that it's a trip
to the moon because it's so wildly impossible?"

"Something like that," he agreed. "It's a reaching for things out of the ordinary grasp. Somehow
he's got to be stopped. Probably he'll stop himself
by trying too hard. But he'll never quit short of
death. He knows what he's up against, and from
now on he'll fight harder than ever."

"You rather admire him, don't you?"

"Yes, I do. I consider him utterly, completely
mistaken—but he believes in what he's doing,
and deeply enough to give his life for it."

"But you don't think he can put it over?"

"I think he might, if he could control everything," Rawls said seriously. "But he's putting his
trust in outlaws at the gold camps, renegades of

the worst kind. I wouldn't trust them for a minute."

Kathleen nodded, and her own understanding
of this man and his methods was broadened. In
him was strength to match that of Mark Whirter,
and in addition he had a vast patience. It could
explode to terrible action on occasion, but he
had a way of letting things work themselves out
—at least, until the moment came to give them
a nudge. She smiled at him, then swung about,
startled, at the heavy tramp of feet.

Whirter stood there. Anger burned in his eyes,
but with it was a sort of obscure satisfaction, as
though, having been goaded to a decision, it
pleased him to know that he was right in taking
it.

"You're going to hate me," he said bluntly, addressing both of them. "Though I venture that
you'll also like what I'm going to do. Find a good
spot for anchoring," he added.

"What's going on?" Rawls asked.

"You'll find out. Come along, both of you."

Once the two packets were at anchor, a safe distance off from shore, in a quiet backwater af-
forded by the lee of an island, he explained.
Astrid was there, looking angry, and Whirter met
her glance with a level unconcern.

"We're going to have a wedding aboard," he said bluntly. "A double wedding, in fact. It's easy to see that you and Miss Garrison are in love with each other, Rawls. Likewise, it has been understood for quite a while that Astrid and I are to marry."

"All that you want of me is to be Lomax McQuestion's son-in-law," Astrid retorted furiously. She had bearded the lion in his den, and she had struck fire—a flame that frightened her now.

"I did want that, once, though it's of no importance now," Whirter replied. "You've been trying to stir up trouble—and with only four women along, and two shiploads of men, and two of the women white, it's easy to have trouble, of a sort that you might not relish."

He spoke with a cold dispassion twice as frightening as anger, gazing from one to the other.

"So I'm taking steps, as a prudent man must, to solve this woman problem. Rawls and I are ship captains, and as such we have the power to marry people. I'll marry you and Miss Garrison, Rawls. You will perform the ceremony for Astrid and myself. Now."

"I certainly have no intention of marrying

you," Astrid snapped, and color burned hot in her cheeks.

She started to say more, then bit her lip and controlled her tongue. But Whirter did not let it go at that. "Why?" he prodded.

"Must you ask?" she demanded. "It's enough that I don't care to."

"If you have any serious objections, I'm willing to listen to them," he conceded. "But on the whole, I think it will be much better to do it my way, now. The others are raising no objections."

Kathleen looked at Rawls. The blood pulsed in her cheeks and throat, but her eyes were steady. Rawls turned.

"Under other conditions, we might be happy to consider it," he said, "but you go too far, Whirter. This is not a matter for force."

"Meaning that you won't?"

"That's the size of it."

"I think you will. Or would you like it better reversed—Astrid to marry Rawls, Kathleen to be my blushing bride?"

Rawls had controlled his anger up to now. But this put a strain on it that was hard to bear.

"Neither the one nor the other," he retorted. "Have you lost your mind, Whirter?"

"It'll be one or the other," Whirter growled,

and his rage was an answering spark. "You and everyone else will do well to get it through your heads that I'm master here. Whatever I think is best for the expedition is what will be done. Perhaps you girls would prefer to be set ashore, instead—where you might find yourselves other lovers?"

Astrid slapped him, a stinging open-handed blow that drove the blood from his face, then sent it flooding back in the finger-marks. Whirter did not move, but his eyes were unpleasant.

"I'll remember that," he promised. "I—"

"Don't try to push us too far," Rawls warned. "There's a limit to what you can get away with."

"I'll show you whether there's any limit to what I can do!" Whirter was beside himself. "If any of you think—"

An interruption came as the door was flung open. Taber, his long face drawn in anxious lines, burst into the room. His voice was hoarse with apprehension.

"McQuestion's dead," he said.

Chapter Nine

The news of McQuestion's passing checked Whirter in mid-stride. With an effort, he resumed his normal composure and took appropriate action. But as the hours wore on it was as though a new book had been opened, an old one tossed aside. Lomax McQuestion had been owner of the *Astrid* and, in theory at least, the head of this expedition.

Now that restraint was removed, and the change was quickly apparent. There had been that same sense of bridges burned behind them when they'd left the Missouri and turned up the Yellowstone. But this time the feeling was stronger, and it extended to everyone. Overnight, the atmosphere grew strained and brittle.

A general assembly was ordered aboard the *Varina* the next morning, to include all who could be spared from the *Astrid's* crew as well.

"We'll have a proper burial service before proceeding," Whirter said. "We still have a long way to go." He opened a Bible, thumbed through it. Taber interrupted.

"Do you mean that we're still going on—after what's happened?" he asked incredulously.

"Going on?" Whirter's eyes were frosty. "Of course. Nothing has happened to change our plans. Nothing will change them."

A protesting murmur ran among the gathered crewmen, and uneasy glances were cast at the not-distant shore, at what the leafy green of trees might conceal. Sol Sherwood hesitated, then backed his partner.

"It sounds to me like a crazy notion, Cap'n, going on when the Injuns are so hostile," he said bluntly. "We never expected nothin' like this when you said you had a job—"

"Shut up!" The words were a sudden roar of pent-up anger. "I'll stand for no back talk from anyone, much less from a bungler like you—"

That was the moment when an arrow came winging out from among the trees, hard-driven. It buried itself in Sherwood's fat throat, so that he staggered and choked, then sought to wrench at it with both hands. As he tugged, crimson gushed suddenly, and he pitched forward on his face, the arrow still quivering.

For a breathless moment there was no sound, while men stared in fascination. No crash of guns or further flight of arrows followed, only that single missive that had been so well aimed.

A count of ten could have been taken over the fallen man while the silence endured. Then, with a choking grunt that was almost a scream, Taber turned and leaped toward Whirter, and a knife gleamed in his hand.

No one saw the gun appear in Whirter's fist. He still held the Bible in the other, and Taber's jump was fast, but not so quick as the gun. As it roared, Taber collapsed, crumpling on the deck almost at Whirter's feet.

Silence followed the echo of the gun blast, rolling off among the hills into a distant mocking whisper. Astrid's hand was at her mouth, but no one spoke. After a moment, Whirter went on, almost as if nothing had happened.

"Mr. Earnshaw, please have these unfortunates prepared for burial, also. We'll use one service for all. And move everyone to the main saloon, as a precautionary measure."

The sudden rage had gone out of him, but it had had its effect. Momentarily, at least, the spirit of revolt was quelled. No one commented as preparations went forward. Whirter prepared to conduct the funeral, placing the Bible on a desk, and ostentatiously laying his revolver beside it. Thumbing for the place he sought, he read a passage, intoning the words solemnly.

"As for man, his days are as grass; as a flower of the field, so he flourisheth.

"For the wind passeth over it, and it is gone; and the place thereof shall know it no more."

He signed to some of the hands as the service was ended, and the canvas-wrapped, weighted bodies were taken out. Whirter closed the book and reached for the gun.

"I've been aware of the talk that's been going on for some time," he said. "Mutinous talk, men saying that it's folly to go on. I'll have no more of it. Those who signed for this enterprise knew that they were embarking upon a risky venture, but it was for home and country. Nothing is altered. Remember that you are under my orders as your superior officer, that your only hope of salvation lies in sticking together and doing as I say.

"Mutiny would bring not alone the savage hordes upon us. Escape from them leaves you in a wilderness, in the enemy country, and out of uniform, where your status is nothing less than that of spies. Keep it in mind that I make the decisions, and that we are going on." He paused, then turned to Rawls. "Mr. Rawls, we will get under way, please. At once."

Rawls had listened to the service, wondering anew what sort of man this was. Now he shook his head.

"I have an idea that we've come far enough. So far as I'm concerned, we certainly have."

"Meaning that you refuse to pilot any more?"

"Upriver, yes."

Whirter's reaction was not quite what the others had expected. He looked at Astrid.

"Have you, by any chance, changed your mind? About marrying me?"

"After you've murdered my father?" Astrid's voice broke on grief and anger. "I should say not!"

Whirter shrugged. His demeanor became icy.

"Unless you pilot us, Mr. Rawls, you become merely excess baggage, an encumbrance aboard and of no possible use to the purposes of this expedition. So I'll give you a choice. You will continue to take these boats upstream, or you will be set ashore, along with the four women of the party. I leave it to you to decide."

The cold-bloodedness of that pronouncement was staggering. Some of the crew looked shocked, but it was plain that they would obey orders. That made Kathleen and Astrid hostages for Rawls' good behavior.

"In that case, we'll try it a while longer," Rawls agreed. "Up-anchor, please, Mr. Earnshaw."

Whirter returned to the *Astrid*, with no further word to anyone. Both boats plowed ahead, the engines racing, paddle wheels churning the water to froth as they sought enough grip to push them along, then slowing to a crawl as Rawls hunted a channel. Several times every day they had to turn back and nose out a new course like a dog sniffing at a new trail, but somehow they managed to keep going.

The thrill of adventure, the hint of romantic endeavor that had sustained the crew up to this point, was gone. They still obeyed orders, but McQuestion's death, the tragic fate of Taber and Sherwood, the callous brutality of Whirter's pronouncement concerning the women, had changed everything. The unyielding hostility of the Indians was matched by the unreasoning fanaticism of the man who had suddenly become a stranger.

Earlier they had laughed at Narcissus and her tea leaves. Now they believed the black woman. There was a cup of trouble that all must drink.

Summer had caught up with them. The days

were long, the sun hot in a cloudless sky. Occasional thunderheads blew up during the afternoons, black and threatening, but they passed with never more than a few scattered drops of rain. The hills took on a brown tint, and the river continued to drop. Picking a channel was like walking a tightrope.

But other boats had come this far upstream in the past. They came upon the wreckage of one, so weathered that it must have been there at least since the previous summer. It lay at the lower point of an island, half-submerged, and they halted for a look.

Not much was left, but Rawls came upon a cannon, half in mud, covered over by drift and wreckage. Apparently it had escaped observation by the Indians, or else they had known of no way to make use of it.

"Hoist it aboard," Rawls instructed, and at Earnshaw's look of incredulity, he explained. "Once it's cleaned and polished, we have powder and we can contrive shrapnel to load it with. It may come in handy."

Earnshaw was dubious. "Are you sure it won't explode and kill the gun crew if it's fired?" he asked.

"That's a possibility," Rawls conceded. "But

also a risk that I'd balance against some others."

"You've got something there," Earnshaw agreed.

A thin cheer went up when finally they reached the Powder. Not a big river at this season of the year, still it made a difference in the amount of water when that much was subtracted as they went on. Here the badlands were beautiful and bizarre, a fitting setting for the nightmare journey they had embarked upon.

Anger was building in Rawls. For himself he didn't particularly care, but holding the women as hostages tied his hands. Whirter had planned it that way from the first, and he was capable of carrying out his threat to get his way.

"It wouldn't be so bad if your boat wasn't involved," Rawls said to Kathleen. "Each day makes a worse situation. Even if we were to turn back, there's no more water going downstream than up, and it takes just so much to float a packet."

"I might feel sorry for myself," Kathleen retorted unexpectedly, "if it wasn't for Astrid. She and I have grown to be good friends, Denny. I feel sorry for her."

"I don't," he said. "She schemed and connived and overreached herself."

"That's all true, but seeing what she was reaching for, I can't blame her too much." And leaving him to mull over that, she moved away.

Here came the Tongue, with the nature of the country beginning to change, a more ordinary landscape on either side. The crew performed their tasks, guns ever at hand, in a silent watchfulness. That this was a journey of folly was increasingly apparent, but Mark Whirter showed no signs of giving up. Rawls knew how the men with Columbus must have felt, convinced that they were approaching the edge of darkness, the drop-off to destruction. Such an atmosphere was here.

Somehow they reached the Big Horn, flowing strong from the south. And Whirter's good nature came back as a horseman appeared and signaled from the shore, a peculiar sideways and up and down motion with his hat.

"We'll drop anchor," Whirter instructed Rawls, though it was still early. "That's the sign I've been waiting for. The Innocents are here with horses for the trip overland. That fellow is one of them."

Having signaled, the messenger withdrew, apparently to wait for night. Watching as the dark made a black ribbon of the river, Rawls saw the man come down to the shore, a shadow merging with the water. He called softly when he reached the *Varina* and was assisted to the deck.

"Thought I'd wait, just to be on the safe side," he explained. "You Mr. Whirter?"

"He's on the other boat," Rawls explained. "We'll send word to him that you're here." He led the way to a cabin.

In the light, the outlaw was not prepossessing. A young man gone to seed too soon. Whiskers sprouted in patches from his face, and the rest of him was in keeping. There was an overbold look in his eyes as he surveyed his surroundings.

"Pretty fine," he said. "You fellers do your-selves well. I'm Slash Jenkyn—lately of Alder Gulch."

Swagger edged the words, but they sounded like an attempt to cover inner nervousness. Whir-ter entered, escorted by Earnshaw. He looked at Rawls as if undecided and then jerked his head.

"You might as well stay," he suggested. "You're in this now with the rest of us." He refrained from adding, Like it or not, and there was an un-certainty that had not been noticeable before. Though too proud to ask, he wanted Rawls' judg-ment.

Jenkyn reintroduced himself, extending his hand.

"I got somethin' here to identify me," he added, and pulled out a letter, wrapped against the wetness. "It's the one you wrote last," he added significantly. "Just to let you be sure that I'm the right feller."

Whirter glanced at it and was satisfied.

"The fact that you're here is proof enough," he said. "You've got the horses?"

"Yeah, some of the boys are holdin' a cavy, back on shore. You fellers know how to ride?" he asked curiously.

"Most of our men were in the cavalry," Whirter explained curtly. "How is everything?"

"Couldn't be better, I reckon. Everybody minin' lots of gold and afraid to ship it out." His smile was crooked. "We've seen to that. When they tried it, it didn't get far, an' neither did them that was takin' it. It'll be rich pickin's."

He explained that his companions were keeping back out of sight, as he had done, until sure of the lay of the land. It paid to be careful, these days.

No fault could be found with that, though there had been no sign of Indians for more than a week, and Jenkyn reported that his party had seen no recent sign. Whirter inclined to the opinion that they had finally grown tired of pursuing two boats that were obviously too strong for a successful attack. Now, with extra men on shore to bolster their party, he was confident of a swift foray overland, a devastating attack on the gold camps, and success.

Daylight brought confirmation of Jenkyn's story. There was a broad open plain here on the southern shore, except for a single clump of cottonwood trees, a couple of acres in extent, a quarter of a mile back from the river. On the open ground appeared a full two hundred head of horses, sleek cayuse stock being herded by half a dozen riders.

"The rest of the boys'll be havin' breakfast back at camp," Jenkyn explained, with a wave to where a wisp of smoke showed. "There's a dozen more of 'em—twenty of us in all. Plenty to make any Injuns think twice, but we didn't aim to take no chances, and we ain't seen ary sign of a redskin all the way here."

"We'll go ashore and get started right away," Whirter decided. Days before, with cool forethought, he had had packs made up for those who would make the trip, small turkeys containing only bare necessities—a blanket, matches, sufficient food, and extra ammunition for the

guns. Each man would carry this on his back until mounted.

Turning back, he picked his men, most of them
eager to volunteer now that prospects looked
bright. Eighty were selected, since that would
give a hundred in all, a force ample for a surprise
raid. That left an extra horse apiece for relays.
Jenkyn assured him that pack horses would be
easy to secure at the camps, for carrying back the
loot.

Earnshaw was left in charge of the boats. Since
the water was scarcely more than waist-deep at
any point between the *Varina* and the shore, they
waded ashore in a body, Whirter and Jenkyn at
their head. The horses were still grazing, half a
mile away.

Rawls watched in silence. Whirter had ignored
him this morning, though no doubt giving Earnshaw instructions regarding him. Now Whirter
was like a small boy let out from school, eager for
adventure. Rawls shook his head.

"Some folks are that trustin' it's surprisin'," he
said. "These Innocents are known outlaws—and
from such signs as they've given us so far, the Indians are plenty hostile. If I was going ashore that
way, I'd drop a shot from the cannon off in that

clump of trees first, just to be sure there wasn't any surprise party planned."

Earnshaw gave him a startled glance, swung to look at the leafy covert of cottonwoods.

"I wouldn't want to stampede the horses," he said. "If everything's all right, we'd get the devil."

"And if it isn't, the devils get them." Rawls shrugged. "It shouldn't bother the horses, way off there. But I don't know why I should worry."

Earnshaw made up his mind. The cannon had been cleaned and polished, a trained crew chosen for its operation. Now, at his orders, they swiveled it around, aiming for the middle of the trees. "Fire away!" he instructed.

The boom of the big gun was a startling salute to the sunrise. For a moment, beyond a rising cloud of smoke from the muzzle, nothing happened. Then, as shrapnel whirled and twisted to earth, the cottonwoods seemed to explode in turn. Wild pandemonium broke among them, shrieks and gobbling yells, then horsemen burst out from the shelter—scores of warriors, terrified by the unexpected and the unknown, seeking only to get away.

Within a matter of minutes, once the men from the boats had gotten well back from the shore, they would have been the objective. Now they were disregarded and forgotten.

With the Indians, heading for the cover of other distant woods at the valley's edge, went the band of cayuses and the herdsmen.

On shore, the others checked in amazement. Whirter watched, his jaw tightening grimly. His voice, brittle as cracking ice above a pond, checked Jenkyn as he started to sidle away.

"One more step and I'll kill you," he warned. "And now, Mr. Jenkyn, if you have anything to say, you'd best talk fast!"

Something of the terror that had beset the bushwackers communicated itself to Jenkyn. His face looked more mottled than before, but his tongue was lively.

"Honest, I didn't have no choice," he whined. "They jumped and grabbed us boys as we was headin' this way, a couple of days ago, an' there was a renegade white with them that read the letter. He figgered this scheme out. I didn't want to do it—only they had the rest of my friends, and they'd have to pay if I didn't." He shivered.

"I figured, with a bunch like we have here, and the others on the boats, we could put up a good fight. But have you ever seen what they do to poor devils when things go wrong? And I reckon they'll work on the other boys now."

He put on a good act, but it came out too patly. Anger still shook Whirter, for it had been a near thing. Few of them would have gotten back to the river if they had kept on. And he had a good idea who had suggested firing that shot—something he should have thought of beforehand.

"I don't like double-crossers," Whirter growled, and mockery reared in his own mind at memory of the part he had played as a spy in the Union Army. "There's one treatment for your kind."

Jenkyn's jaws worked slackly. Then he tried again.

"If you're thinkin' about the hosses, they wouldn't have done you no good—not even if we'd got to the diggings. Things ain't the way they was at the gold camps, not these days. I tell you I didn't have no choice, between the Injuns on the one hand and the Vigilantes on the other."

"Vigilantes? Who are they?"

"Ain't you heard? The miners kind of got fed up with the way us Innocents was doing, during the winter. So some of them got together to stop us, and they call themselves the Vigilantes. Men like Colonel Sanders organized them, and they hung a score or so of us fellers. Even hung the sheriff. So if you got that far, you wouldn't have found any friends left to help out."

"I'm amazed that these Vigilantes didn't hang you while they were about it!" Whirter said caustically.

"They would have if I hadn't got out of town, and that part of the country, two jumps ahead of them," Jenkyn confessed. "I headed this way, with a few of the other boys, figgerin' you'd be along. Then the Injuns caught us, like I said. That didn't leave me no choice but to do what I did. But I did risk my neck, first off, to try and get here an' warn you how things was."

Whirter had a pretty good idea of how much truth was mixed with deception in the story. In all likelihood, the part about the Vigilantes was true, but he doubted the rest. He hesitated, the tough side of his mind again at work, refusing to admit defeat.

They had returned to the river bank, and now they waded back to the boats and clambered aboard.

"Lock him up," Whirter instructed, indicating the crestfallen Jenkyn. "I suppose you'll want to go deeper into this, Captain Rawls," he added, and swung away as Jenkyn was hustled below.

That last phrase sprang of deliberate intention. Already he had heard sufficient comment to know that it was Rawls who had suggested the shot that had saved them. Under these circumstances, with his hair intact, he knew that he should feel gratitude, and in turn he should give up his wild project and throw himself upon Rawls' mercy.

The knowledge of a right course grated roughly against the increasing anger he felt for Rawls. Time and again, Denny Rawls, the paragon of this north country, had made a fool of him, and had saved him from the consequences of his own folly. And this time, though he owed his life to what Rawls had done, it was particularly bitter. The fact that he was in the wrong did nothing to relieve pent-up hatred.

He wasn't licked yet. Getting horses and going overland to attack the gold camps was out of the question. Lack of trustworthy guides was a complication, and the organized and tough-minded Vigilantes would seem such an added hazard as to rule out all chance of success. Unless—and the idea that had come to him seemed worth a gamble.

Jenkyn was a scoundrel, first an outlaw and an Innocent, then, whether the story he had told was true or not, a double-crosser, as Whirter had accused. But why boggle at words when he was doing it all for a principle that was still at stake? Jenkyn might be useful.

Everyone was gabbling excitedly about what had happened. That furnished the opportunity he was seeking to slip away. Five minutes later, Whirter let himself in to the 'tween-decks cabin where Jenkyn had been thrown.

"I've got to talk fast," Whirter said, lowering his voice and glancing furtively around. "If Rawls found out about me being here, he'd raise the devil."

"I thought you was in command," Jenkyn retorted dubiously.

"I was," Whirter acknowledged. "But he's pulled so many things like that one with the cannon that the crew are ready to follow him, not me. But if he gets control, it'll go hard with both of us. And there's more than one way to skin a cat. If a bunch of us were to hit the gold camps hard and sudden—like we'd planned—isn't there plenty of gold to make it worth while?"

A gleam returned to Jenkyn's eyes. "Gold!" he repeated. "Those camps are lousy with it! But you ain't got a chance of reachin' them. And if you did, it'd take a big crew to get anywhere. Them miners will put up a hell of a fight."

"Let them! We'll have the crew, and a big one. I suppose you and your Indian friends know all about what happened downriver. But however it may sound, the Sioux are making a mistake. I'm their friend."

"Yeah? After what just happened, they'll sure think so!"

Whirter checked the hot retort that rose to his lips at the sneer. It told him exactly where Jenkyn stood.

"You know that I didn't have anything to do about that order—though I'm glad the cannon was fired, with you and them set to double-cross us. But there's been mistakes on both sides, and that trouble back in Dakota was another case where Rawls and McQuestion double-crossed them.

"I brought the guns and the whiskey along, all the way from St. Louis, because I wanted the Sioux to have them," Whirter went on impatiently. "Can't you see? I'm an officer of the Confederacy. So we're on the same side, if they'd only believe it. Well, you're one of them. We can work together—if they have any sense."

Jenkyn had envisioned the rope for the part he had played. Any respite was welcome.

"Go ahead," he said hoarsely. "You can count on me!"

Chapter Ten

"It's a matter of common sense and self-interest for everybody concerned," Whirter explained. "There's a lot of whiskey aboard these boats—enough to cough up the war whoops in every Indian gullet west of the Mississippi! We've also got a lot of guns. It was McQuestion's idea to trade them for furs.

"So far as I'm concerned, I don't want to trade the stuff for fur—just for friendship and good-will. In other words, if I get you loose from here, your job will be to tell the Indians that they can have the guns and whiskey—all of it—for nothing. That ought to prove that I'm on their side."

"How much is there?" Jenkyn asked hoarsely.

"About enough to make up the cargo of one boat. I'll have it all transferred to the *Astrid*, and we'll take it upriver another day's run, then unload it for them. I'll expect them to drink the liquor and to use the guns to the best advantage.

And if you have any influence with them, why shouldn't they go along with me to raid those gold camps? They can have everything they find—including scalps—everything except the gold. I want that. But they'll get big value for their share."

Jenkyn drew a deep breath. Whirter was a man with a mind that could not be swerved from an idea, and as usual, he made that seem a plausible notion. For his own part, knowing something of the men at Alder Gulch, at Virginia City and other near-by camps, Jenkyn had no desire to approach any closer to them than he now was, no matter what the inducement. Besides, though that was his secret, he had other fish to fry. There was a lot of difference between theory and practice—particularly when the latter was emphasized by the noose.

And he knew that the Indians felt pretty much as he did. Red Cloud and his warriors had a long list of grievances against the white man, and with a handful of renegades to egg them on, they were causing considerable of a ruckus. But Red Cloud was a canny warrior. That he'd like to get the guns went without dispute, and his men would like the whiskey.

But they wouldn't be interested in an expedi-

tion against such long odds as this one represented. It was one thing for Whirter to plan a
quick surprise attack and then a swift withdrawal
with the loot, an escape out of the country. For
him it might work. For them it could only mean
a running battle increasing in fury as the miners
and other settlers rallied. And in the end it could
mean only disaster.

Jenkyn considered this, but he cannily refrained from voicing it aloud. Whirter aimed to
use him for a tool. It might be that the process
could be reversed.

Whirter talked, outlining plans in swift detail.
Jenkyn nodded agreement.

"I'll smuggle you ashore as soon as it's dark,"
Whirter added. "You do your part, and everybody will profit in a big way. The fact that I'll risk
putting myself in the hands of the Indians, along
with delivering the guns and liquor, should
prove my good faith. And there's one other
thing."

"Yeah?"

"We've got to get rid of Rawls. After today,
he'd maybe influence the men, and we can't have
any dissension. When the time comes, I want him
killed. He always wears a red jacket—and he's

the only man who has one. That should make it easy."

"I'll tend to that," Jenkyn agreed.

Whirter returned to the deck. The excitement had abated, the new topic of conversation was about exhausted, and they again looked to him, expectantly. His face told them nothing.

"We had a close shave this morning," he said. "I see now that it was a mistake to go ashore before the cannon was fired to test them out. But with Mr. Earnshaw obeying orders to the letter, it worked out very well." A glance at Earnshaw showed his face expressionless, and Whirter knew that, put that way, Earnshaw would continue to obey. He was a soldier first, and so were these others.

"War," he went on, "is a game in which only one thing counts—the final battle. It doesn't matter how many skirmishes you lose if you win the final victory. If you can't succeed by a frontal attack, try a rear-guard action. But win. That's what we're going to do."

He looked around, rapped out his orders.

"Mr. Earnshaw, please have the cargoes of both boats partially changed. I want the whiskey and guns, except for enough to arm the men who will remain with the *Varina,* transferred at once to the *Astrid,* and the other stuff aboard her shifted to the *Varina.* As soon as that's done, we're going on, as far upriver as it's possible to take the *Astrid.* I figure that we can reach Pomp's Pillar. The *Varina* will remain here with the women and a sufficient crew to protect her, with you in charge. As for the rest of us, when we can go no farther by boat, we'll strike overland, attain our objective, and return.''

Cannily he refrained from explaining what he really had in mind, but Rawls had no difficulty in guessing. Taking the whiskey as well as the guns made that clear. If anything, this was a bigger gamble than before, but Whirter was a gambler at heart. And it was those all-or-nothing stakes that occasionally paid off.

The men were dubious, but they set to work under Earnshaw's direction. Whirter had given the impression that he had ordered the cannon to be fired, and that helped restore their confidence. The very daring of the idea, as he outlined it, appealed to them, a challenge to the fighter in every man. Once more they'd go along.

It was no surprise to Rawls to find, in the morning, that Jenkyn had made his escape. The cargo had been transferred, and now the *Astrid* prepared to pull out, leaving her sister ship behind. Rawls, as usual, was at the wheel.

"If you try any tricks," Whirter warned him grimly, "I'll shoot you. I would follow such a course with regret, mindful of the very real services you have rendered us. But I count the Cause bigger than you or myself or all of us put together. Make no mistake about that."

He meant it, as Rawls knew. But he'd made up his own mind as completely. This had gone far enough—the *Astrid*, the whole rash scheme. Mad as it had been, Whirter had gotten this far, and he might manage to win. Once embarked overland, his men would have no other choice than to back him to the limit, fighting like devils when called upon to do so. If the Indians were convinced that he was on their side, they might wipe out the gold camps, and go on from there to such an orgy of terror as Whirter had first conceived, while Whirter made a run back downriver with the loot that he hoped would revive the faltering Confederacy.

No one could deny that Whirter was giving all he had, risking his life at every turn, for something in which he believed. Now that Kathleen was fairly safe, Rawls knew that he could do no less. When Earnshaw became convinced that disaster had overtaken the *Astrid,* he would take the *Varina* back to the Missouri, if it were humanly possible to do so. Loaded now with the proper cargo for Fort Benton, Earnshaw would get it there if he could.

There was still one way to put a stop to Whirter's ambitious plan. If the *Astrid* was run hard aground, so solidly that it could not be gotten off, the Indians would think of the loot of guns and whiskey ready for the taking. And in their present mood, they'd take!

It had to be done today, before the meeting could be held and an alliance worked out with Whirter. Rawls had no illusions as to his own chances, once he wrecked the *Astrid.* Like the others, he wouldn't be going back.

He'd tried to find Kathleen for a last word, in the darkness before dawn, before transferring to the *Astrid.* In the confusion, he hadn't been able to locate her. There had not been much time. Perhaps it was as well, but it was hard to come to the end of a dream, to know that the awakening of cold reality had forever shattered it.

He could almost feel her beside him, as she had stood so many times, watching the river, the moving shores in ever-changing panorama. It seemed as if he could smell the perfume that he always associated with her, a subtle fragrance, bewitching as her quick smile.

This was no dream. He grew cold with realization, finding her beside him.

"You don't seem glad to see me, Denny," Kathleen murmured. "Am I as dreadful as the glimpse of a Sioux?"

"How can I feel glad about you being here, thinking of the Sioux?" he asked. "On the *Varina,* you at least had a chance. That was the one thing that made this journey easier for me, the hope that you might come out all right."

"Meaning that you didn't expect to come back? Do you think it would seem right to me, in that case?" There was no coquetry here, but a realization of facts and a frank facing of them. "I like it better this way, Denny. I'd have come along, even if it hadn't been suggested that I should."

So Whirter had been responsible. She saw the trouble in his face, and her own voice was steady.

"You spoke as though we were getting toward the end of something—to the river's end, perhaps. I'm not asking what you meant. But whatever you were going to do, you must go ahead, just the same. Nothing can be allowed to make any difference. What must be done is bigger than we are, Denny."

He was silent, staring ahead, unmindful of the sharp upthrust of boulders from the river bottom, of the torn froth of the current, so like his own mind. She had made a declaration of more than faith, and her willingness to be with him in such a situation was both uplifting and depressing. His rage at Whirter threatened to turn from chill to explosive flame. Urging Kathleen to this journey was proof that the man had cast aside all qualms, that he now would stop at nothing to get his way.

Rawls had planned to run the *Astrid* hard aground and be done without delay. Now his hands on the wheel were clammy with sweat, and they continued to creep upriver, the hours wearing by, his mind a torment. He noted landmarks mechanically, out of long habit. It would be better to wait until night was close at hand, now that Kathleen was along. That would increase the distance back to the *Varina,* and lengthen the hazards of reaching it, but any escape from a stranded boat would be impossible by daylight.

Clouds came with the afternoon, piling dark against the horizon, torn by lightning. For some miles the river had been deep and sluggish, but now it hurried as if impatient to reach some secret rendezvous. The engines made frenzied labor, driving against the sharpness of the current.

A couple of hundred feet upstream, Rawls saw what he had been waiting for, half hoping not to find. The outlines were sharply etched; the fluted water turning to an angry boil as it slid past told his experienced eyes the exact quality of the obstruction. This was a knifelike rock, and once on that, there would be no getting the *Astrid* off again. Even if grasshoppering was possible, the bottom would be sliced out.

Kathleen had returned to the pilothouse. Rawls looked at her, marveling at the serenity of her face as she gave him a quick smile, feeling his own torn and twisted, but knowing that the moment could not be compromised. His eyes ranged the shores, where once more the cottonwoods came close to the banks, shivering to the surge of the wind. The engines, driving at full speed, seemed almost to scream—

For an instant he didn't know what had happened. It was too big, too fraught with confusion, a wild wrenching and twisting as though the boat had been caught in giant hands that were tearing it apart while it screamed in agony, an ear-shattering sound. The razor edge of the rock was still ahead, and then, as he was flung violently backward and the hiss of escaping steam rose like the shriek of devils, Rawls understood. The long-overstrained boilers had burst.

He found himself in the water, surrounded by parts of the disintegrating packet. The explosion had torn it apart, smashing with relentless power, and already fire was racing to take over what the spite of the steam had left.

This was not at all as Rawls had pictured such an event in his mind. It had happened with such speed that the pilothouse had been torn loose and flung aside, along with whatever happened to be on it. Most of the *Astrid* had not fared so well, nor had the others aboard her. But his thought still was for Kathleen. She had been beside him—

Debris was everywhere, coating the river in a tangled jumble, making it hard to pick out individual objects. Something stirred in the water, and he swam that way, grabbed at a thrashing arm, whitely upflung. Kathleen's head came out of the water, hair streaming, her eyes wide and dazed. Her fingers found his own wrist and tightened convulsively, but it was a possessive clutch, free of panic.

Only now was the full effect of the disaster beginning to appear. There was a curious lack of screams and cries, testifying to the swift destructiveness of the first blast. The tormented noise of wood and metal shrieked in final disintegration, the crackle of flames rising as the other subsided.

From the shores the silence remained unbroken, but several figures came into view, like phantom spirits conjured out of hell; men who moved soundlessly and watched half in bewilderment, half in avid expectancy. The startling end of the *Astrid* had taken the Indians as much by surprise as anyone, and they had not yet adjusted themselves to the full meaning of the disaster, to the fact that the whiskey and the guns were gone.

Some of that daze gripped Rawls, as though this was a dream from which he must presently awaken. He saw a warrior wade out from shore, slipping once and almost falling, but going with methodical purpose. About him in this moment was none of the theatrical pomp of blazing attack, yet he was doubly sinister as he caught something that floated and started dragging a dead man to shore for the dreadful business of securing a trophy.

Most of the crew must have perished in the explosion. For the others there would be no mercy if they reached the bank, and the thought dispelled the fog in Rawls' mind, jerked him back to reality. He must reach shore with Kathleen—

The water ran swiftly, deep with a glassy surface, marred by the jumble of debris. That wreckage might give them a chance. In the confusion and with the multiplicity of objects that dotted the surface, it was long odds if anyone on shore had seen them. Here came something apt to their need—a big, upholstered lounging chair from one of the saloons, a touch of downriver elegance, floating upside down.

It wasn't hard to reach and duck beneath it, to get a hold on the ornate buttons that fastened the tufted stuffing, and cling there. Kathleen was relaxed as if partly dazed, and when they didn't struggle, it took only a little effort to keep afloat.

There was an air space under the chair above the water, room enough where the arm curved for Rawls to look out at the side. With his vision restricted, he could get only a confused glimpse of the shore, but the current was carrying them toward it. Salvation and disaster.

The balance between the two was thin. The Sioux had swarmed along the shore for weeks, keeping out of sight but having no particular difficulty in following as fast as the boats traveled. Today they had been waiting in anticipation of the booty promised when the *Astrid* should stop for the night. Now, all need for concealment gone, they were eager for any fragment of treasure that might be washed within their reach.

Rawls kicked, striving to fight the strong tug of the current and keep their ungainly shelter farther out, but the big chair was growing logy with water, as impossible of management as a ship without a rudder. It wouldn't be long before it would settle to the bottom, but meanwhile it would take its own course.

It hit a jutting boulder with a dull thud, caught and hung, tipping partly up on one side, down on the other. Under them the water was shallow enough to crouch on the bottom, heads above the current, and with the chair tipped the view was wider, though scarcely better. It revealed a score of Indians along the shore, some wading out to grab at such articles as looked inviting, none of them more than a stone's throw away.

A hoarse shout broke the uncanny silence that had followed the first disaster. Not far upstream a man struggled for footing as the piece of wreckage to which he had been clinging swept to where the water shallowed. He stood up, floundering like an ungainly, crippled bird, all but losing his footing in the pull of the current. That he was hurt and dazed was apparent. That it was Mark Whirter was harder to believe, for he looked a crimson scarecrow.

The explosion had torn most of the clothes off Whirter, leaving him clad only in his underwear —a long red garment now torn and flapping. But he had survived this far, and now, shouting again, he splashed through the shallow water toward the beach.

A score of feet out, he halted uncertainly, passing a hand dazedly across his eyes. It was his final gesture, for one of the warriors hurled a tomahawk. Almost before it had struck, he rushed out to grab his victim and drag him toward the shore.

Kathleen gasped and turned her head away, and Rawls, feeling sick, realized that the shock was passing from her mind—the original shock. This one was almost as bad. Most of the Indians clustered about the object on the sand, then drew back as the victorious warrior stood up with his trophy and shook it triumphantly. He gobbled a few words at another man who had just come up and was watching with disapproval. Jenkyn.

Rawls understood the language.

"Here is his hair," the Sioux shouted at Jenkyn. "The man in red!"

It was apparent that the outlaw did not speak Indian. Another man translated.

Understanding came to Rawls. His own red jacket was gone, but if the freakish nature of the explosion had torn it off him as it flung him far out into the river, so had that same prank of the blast revealed Whirter in red. Confirmation was in Jenkyn's reply.

"Yeah, you red sons of Belial killed him, all right. But you got the wrong feller. Seems like his own trap caught him, wearin' red underwear the way he did. Though I reckon it don't make much diff'rence now."

It required more explanation before they understood. So far as the hair hunter was concerned, a trophy was a trophy, but some of the others were disgruntled. Only now were they beginning to realize the full magnitude of what had happened—that guns and whiskey alike were lost, that most of the crew had perished and beyond yielding even a scalp; also any expedition for gain had vanished with the wreckage. All of which left them as losers.

Anger came with knowledge, and part of it was turned against Jenkyn, whom they seemed to feel was somehow responsible for the manner in which things had worked out. They had sent him to the *Varina* in the first place to entice the white men ashore and into their hands, and as the crew had trooped on to the bank a cannon had rained death among them, trained on their place of ambush. They'd given Jenkyn a second chance on his assurances that a mistake had been made, that everything was coming their way. This was the meagre result.

Panic gripped Jenkyn as he sensed their hostility. His words were clearly audible above the suck and gurgle of the current.

"Hold yore hosses, now," he protested, addressing himself to the one warrior who seemed to understand English. "Don't go blamin' me 'cause a boiler busted. You don't figger they aimed to kill themselves, do you? An' if you want booty, and a lot of scalps, you can still get them. There's that other boat, back downriver. Nothin' to hinder going back and getting it. It won't be hard to do, now."

That caught their attention, as he had hoped.

The leaders of the expedition, the men they needed to fear during an assault, were gone, dead. Now the *Varina* could be taken by surprise, and it should be an easy prey, along with all on board, including the women.

"Two of the women are black," he added, knowing the fascination that either black men or women had for most of the Indians, partly because so few of them had ever seen a Negro. "White women, too," he added, "but mighty purty."

They liked the idea when it was explained to them, but there was no rush to put it into execution. The *Varina* would wait. Meanwhile, as long as daylight lasted, the current was washing wreckage to them, and it was worth looking at.

That was the worst of it, as Rawls calculated. For a couple of warriors, the conference ended, were wading hopefully out to have a look at this chair that had stuck here.

Chapter Eleven

Kathleen looked at Rawls. Her gaze remained calm, with no hint of panic. For the first time he noticed that her right arm hung limp at her side.

"How are you?" he demanded. "Are you hurt badly?"

She shook her head. "Only my arm. I think it's broken. That—doesn't matter."

He ran his fingers over it in quick testing, shook his head in relief.

"I don't think there are any bones broken," he said. Apparently she had taken a hard blow that had numbed it, and it was swelling above the elbow, but it could have been much worse.

"We've got to kick loose and trust to luck," he added, and setting his feet against the boulder, he shoved hard, pushing with his shoulders against the sodden weight of the chair. It hesitated, swung, and was floating again, still above

216

them. The Indians would figure that the current had moved it.

Twice, the swirl of the river tried to shove them toward shore, but working together they managed to push it off and keep going. Then the deeper, swifter current caught them, and for a quarter of a mile they were hurried along. The chair was becoming so waterlogged that it was settling steadily, losing its buoyancy so that clinging to it would no longer hold them up.

"We've got to leave it and trust to luck," Rawls said, his voice booming strange and muffled. Kathleen had one arm over his shoulder, his was about her waist to assist her, and once again he was struck by her steadiness in the face of peril. She'd do to ride this or any other river with!

For a second time, with a soft jar, the chair struck an obstruction, tried to settle lower. They crawled from beneath it, heads cautiously above the water, then Rawls straightened. Luck was still giving them an occasional nod. They were standing in waist-deep water, but the current had carried them to the south bank of the river, and here it barely moved; trees and brush on shore overhung the bank and had them in its shelter.

A better covert could not have been planned. But they had been in the water nearly an hour, and they were becoming chilled. The sun was setting, going down behind high hills that edged the valley. Rawls waited a while, using eyes and ears, but there was no alien sound, so he boosted Kathleen up on to the bank, then crawled after her.

Again they waited while the dusk deepened, but most of the Indians were busy farther upstream where the current swirled with wreckage. Some of them had gone out to what remained of the *Astrid,* where they prowled like alley cats.

"What do we do now?" Kathleen asked.

"We'll have to get horses," Rawls explained. "They should have some around somewhere. Can you ride?"

Her low laugh was a trifle shaky. "I used to think I was a pretty fair horsewoman. But I never tried an Indian pony without a saddle."

"Or even a decent apology for a bridle? But I guess you can do anything you have to."

He led the way, circling back from the water, heading upstream. Exercise warmed them, and they had one big advantage. The Indians were sure that there were no survivors, so they wouldn't be on guard. Night closed down, moonless for the first several hours, and that was perfect for their purpose.

Rawls knew this country in a general way. The

Yellowstone ran in a broad easy sweep east and a bit north, and here, beyond the badlands, the valley often widened a lot, then closed again. But getting back to the *Varina,* going overland, would present as many problems in its way as nursing the *Astrid* upstream had done. Now and again the river was pinched between sharply rising bluffs, or else the trees and underbrush grew so thickly that it would be a nightmare passage through them. At such places they'd have to climb the hills to the south and follow the higher open ground.

One other thing was in their favor. Though the engines of the *Astrid* had labored mightily all during the day, they hadn't covered many miles. The winding stream, swift current, and the frequent necessity to hesitate, back up, and nose along for a new channel, had taken time.

But the Indians, eager for loot and scalps, would soon be heading downstream as well. To save themselves and those on the *Varina,* they must reach it without delay.

Though unfamiliar with this particular country, Rawls knew the general terrain, and he understood the habits of the Sioux. He had no trouble, moving carefully and using his ears, in locating some of their cayuses, left hobbled in a little meadow some distance back from the river.

A score of horses were there, and careful scouting failed to disclose any guard. Since this valley swarmed with Sioux, and they were sure that there were no enemies anywhere about, caution was relaxed. It was a long way to any white settlement—over two hundred miles in a straight line to the gold camps of Virginia City or Alder Gulch, and considerably farther to Fort Benton in the north. Salt Lake City was far to the south.

This country had been promised the Indians, and trespass of the whites had infuriated them. Ever since the winter snows had melted, Red Cloud's warriors had been in process of reclaiming this vast stretch of wilderness, driving out or killing the few who had been so daring or foolhardy as to venture into forbidden territory. The two river craft had been the main exceptions, and one of those, with its crew, was no longer in existence.

Rawls moved quietly among the horses, grunting a low word in Indian, as their owners would do. A few reared away but there was no great fright, and he selected two, twisted rawhide about their jaws expertly, and removed the hobbles. The simple rawhide bridles that the Indians used had been conveniently on the branch of a tree at the edge of the meadow.

His air of confidence impressed the horses, but he was under no delusions. Most Indian ponies were rarely more than half broken. It required expert horsemen to ride them, and in that the Sioux were masters. If the Blackfeet were the Red Lords of the Rockies, the warlike Sioux were the possessors of the plains, their prowess equal to their empire.

Leaving one pony with Kathleen, Rawls swung on to the back of the other, clamping his knees. He'd ridden Indian horses before, and he knew how to manage them. This cayuse was unusually tractable, probably because it showed signs of having been ridden far already today. He turned back to where Kathleen waited.

"I think you can ride this one without much trouble," he said, and explained the method of controlling it, mostly with the knees and a mere touch of the single rein. "How is your arm?"

"I can use it a little," Kathleen said.

He boosted her up, noted with approval how quickly she jerked her wet skirt up and clasped the pony with shapely legs; then he was on the other cayuse. He had to do his best riding, for this pony recognized him as alien and was not so tractable. It bucked and pitched and tried to run headlong through the brush and under low limbs of cottonwoods, hoping to scrape him off, but Rawls soon convinced it that he was master.

Kathleen was having no trouble. But a wild yell from behind testified that someone had returned and found two of the horses missing.

To wait around would be more risky than to keep moving under cover of darkness. Luck had been with them these last hours. The pilothouse had proved to be about the safest place on the ill-fated *Astrid,* for it had been blown off into deep water almost intact, taking them with it. Since then, fortune had attended their trail, but they'd need a lot more.

Several times during the night they heard other riders, but a haze of cloud blotted away the stars and blanked out the late-rising moon. It was a friendly dark to that extent, but a hindrance when it came to picking a trail. More than once they reached a blank wall of the river, tangled brush, or a cliff at valley's edge, and were forced to turn back and search out a new course. It was a weary ride as the night grew old, and when day finally came, their horses seemed as tired as themselves.

But they dared not stop. Rawls guessed that they were now ahead of the Indians, who would probably stop for a few hours of sleep, not figuring that there was any great hurry. But there were apt to be other Sioux anywhere along the valley, and those behind would soon be coming, making better time than they could hope to do, because of knowing the trails. To wait for night would be safer, but time was too precious.

"It's only a few more miles, so we'll risk it," Rawls decided.

"How can you tell?"

"Landmarks," he explained. "A pilot always notices them as he goes along, and he has to train himself to remember them. A hill there, which looks like a crouching lion. A dead tree, an island, two boulders at the edge of the river . . . It's like some people reading a book. You glance at a few words, and they tell you what has happened and what is going to happen at that particular place in the book—that is, if you've read it before. See that point ahead? That high bluff with a red scar on its side? We were opposite it when you joined me in the pilothouse yesterday. As soon as we get around it, we'll see the *Varina*."

"It doesn't look far," Kathleen said hopefully.

"Maybe two miles, in a straight line. It'll take us a good hour. Tired?"

She shifted her position wearily, but managed to smile at him.

"I never supposed that a fairly fat horse could be so hard. I used to think a leather saddle was bad—but this is no improvement."

"You're doing fine," he said. "And here's some breakfast."

He reined alongside a tall currant bush, its branches drooping with golden fruit, and snapped off several branches, passing some of them to her. The fruit was sweet and tasty, but scarcely filling after so many hours without other food.

"It will help to stay our stomachs till we can get a meal on the *Varina*." Rawls sighed. "One thing, once we're back aboard, there'll be no one to argue against heading for Fort Union and then up to Benton as fast as we can travel. And the current will be with us as far as Union."

"It sounds like heaven." Kathleen sighed. "And to have Narcissus comb my hair again—what a job she'll have to get the tangles out of it! I must look a sight!"

Rawls eyed her approvingly. "You do," he agreed. "A sight for sore eyes. The only thing that would look any better, under these circumstances, is the *Varina*."

They fell silent again, pushing through trees and brush. From the decks of the *Varina*, these had looked like a cool green covert, a pleasant place on a hot day, but the sun was getting hot again and insects were stirring to activity, rising from the deep grass as a torment. The brush held them back, and there were a thousand hindrances.

But the bluff was close at hand, and there had been no sign of any of the Indians so far today. Kathleen found herself unconsciously leaning forward, her knees gripping the cayuse more tightly as they came down to the river bank where the bluff crowded and then worked around it.

Below, for a couple of miles, the river ran straight, a sheen of silver. But it was an empty river, save for a vanishing smudge of smoke on the lower horizon. The *Varina* was heading downstream, already miles ahead.

Their ponies stopped, glad of any excuse to rest, heads drooping, too tired even to sink their muzzles to the water that lapped about their feet. Kathleen's gaze, crowded with dismay, lifted to Rawls. It was impossible to wipe the consternation from his own face.

"They're gone!" Kathleen whispered.

Reality was not to be brushed aside or blinked away. Out at mid-stream, a long stone's throw away, they had left the *Varina* at anchor the day before. There it had waited out the day and night, making a start not more than an hour ago. The vanishing smoke on the horizon told that.

It was hard. They had counted on the possibility that the Indians might be here, even making an attack, but the notion of the *Varina* being gone had not occurred to them.

Yet a moment's reflection showed Rawls how natural and sensible that was. There had been a lot of wreckage from the *Astrid,* drifting on the current. The water would have been littered with it during the night, and even now some was to be seen, a few scattered bits going past, while other pieces had swept in to shore and found lodgment.

Enough had come to tell Earnshaw what had happened. Nothing short of boilers blowing up could have smashed the *Astrid* in such fashion. That was proof that the *Astrid* would not be returning—nor her crew.

There was a possibility that survivors might make their way downstream, but it was not a probability. Earnshaw would weigh that scant chance against the certainty that the Indians, cheated of the treasure that had been promised them, would think this one more in the long series of tricks that had defrauded them, and would lose no time in attacking the *Varina*. Knowing it now shorthanded, with no second crew to come to their rescue, the Sioux would make an all-out effort.

No blame could attach to Earnshaw. Any fair-minded man would commend him. On the other hand, that vanishing smudge of smoke was like the final mists of hope.

This left them stranded in the heart of a hostile wilderness, without food, weapons, or supplies. Moreover, the tracks of the horses, the broken currant bushes would be seen and read by the Sioux. Breaking those branches had been careless, but an hour ago it hadn't seemed to matter. Now that hour had changed the face of destiny.

Rawls kneed his horse ahead, back toward the shore.

"Nothing to do but keep going," he said tightly. "We aren't licked yet."

Kathleen tried to smile, but it was a twisted effort. "Have we got a chance?" she asked.

"Earnshaw's a good captain, but he's not much of a pilot. He may run her aground any time. If he does, we'll catch up."

That was a chance, but he didn't rate it high.

If they had food and fresh horses, their prospects wouldn't be so dark. By cutting across country where the river made a big bend, they might overtake the *Varina*. But their cayuses had traveled a day and a night, and they were spent.

If they didn't overtake the boat— But it was a thought from which he sheered away. This was summer, and under ordinary conditions he wouldn't be dismayed at the notion of making his way overland as far as Fort Benton or Union, or back to the mining camps. Mountain men had made such trips before, with the hazards heavy against them.

But now the land was swarming with hostiles, and Kathleen, for all her courage, was only a girl. Flies and mosquitoes were a torment. His own pony snorted and swerved away from a clump of grass—from something that sent up a chill buzz of warning, the implacable sound continuing until they were well past. Rattlesnake. There'd be a lot hereabouts, turning ugly as the season of blindness came upon them.

Here was open valley again, save for a scattering of trees or clumps of brush. From behind them came a gobbling sound hatefully familiar— the war whoop. They'd been sighted, and looking back, Rawls saw a dozen horsemen coming.

They were still a quarter of a mile away, but that gap would close fast. Rawls kicked and lashed their own ponies to a run, but the cayuses behind were fresh.

The terrain was rougher here, the formerly flat field broken by gullies, studded with patches of brush and trees like the ragged whiskers on Jenkyn's face.

"Drop off!" Rawls commanded, and suited the action to the word, sliding from his own pony, leaving them to run. As a ruse it might gain a little time, but the dead-tired horses wouldn't go far. They'd soon be seen and the trick discovered.

Kathleen followed his example, and, clutching her hand, Rawls dodged among the brush of a draw. They had come less than a mile from where the *Varina* had lain at anchor.

The riders swept by at a furious gallop, not yet aware of what had happened.

This was fairly good country in which to hide. Rawls moved carefully, picking a course that would leave no sign. A shout of fury and disappointment announced that their trick had been discovered. Silence followed. The hunt was on.

Here was the end of a blind trail. Rawls had believed that this coulee led straight down to the river, to the deeper cluster of trees and brush that shrouded the shores. But it ended abruptly in a sheer bank a dozen feet high, about which brush grew thickly. Beyond was open ground, covered only by grass, so short and sunbaked that even by crawling they couldn't wriggle through without quickly being spotted.

Searchers were close. They could see three men, and one forced his horse into the draw, started down it. They shrank closer against the bank, barely concealed by the thin fringe of leaves. He'd be sure to look into this particular patch before going on.

Now the Sioux was only a score of feet from them, still coming on. He rode and managed the cayuse with his knees, leaving both hands free, and he was a good example both of a horseman and a warrior—tall, handsome in an ugly sort of fashion, a tomahawk ready for instant use, black eyes missing nothing. Rawls clenched his hands, sweating. The horseman wouldn't get close enough for him to use his hands, and even if he did, the Indian would be sure to give a yell before he could throttle him—

The warrior slowed as the brush grew denser, kicked angrily at the stubborn cayuse. Another step and he couldn't fail to see—

The sharp burr of a rattler rasped on Rawls'

overtaut nerves, and he felt the tremor that went through Kathleen, standing close beside him, but she did not jump or cry out, though the sound seemed to come from right at their feet. Still, it wasn't quite that bad. The rattler was a bit farther away, and Rawls managed to make it out—coiled and vicious, shaking tail and flattened gaping head almost on a level, blending so well with the sticks and stones that it was hard to distinguish. Its attention was for the horse and rider.

The cayuse snorted and reared back. Its rider grumbled sharply under his breath, but from where he rode he could not see the rattler, and he had no more stomach for fooling with it in such a spot than did his mount. Convinced by its presence that no one could be hiding here, he allowed the pony to swing around.

For full five minutes they crouched, scarcely breathing. The cadence of the reptile slowed, grew still, then it slithered away. The horses of the searchers had finished with this section and carried their riders to fresh fields. A breeze stirred the grass and leaves overhead, and peace, at least in its outer manifestations, returned to the valley.

The next half-hour dragged. There was a chance of a hidden watcher who would be alert for any movement, but they had to risk that. Moving as carefully as possible, they got to the trees and headed for the river. Here was a welcome half-darkness, pleasantly cool, but thick with mosquitoes.

The Indians wouldn't spend much time looking for them, for the warriors were eager to overtake the *Varina,* each anxious to be in at the kill.

Just ahead, among the screen of trees, something moved. They tensed, then watched with increasing wonder. There was a man there, but he seemed furtive, as anxious as themselves to escape observation.

"He looks like a white man!" Kathleen whispered.

"Jenkyn!" Rawls replied, and his fingers on her arm cautioned silence.

The Innocent had returned almost to the spot where he had first appeared to signal the *Varina.* Now he was on foot, leading two horses. Both were bridled and saddled, and Rawls' eyes gleamed at the sight. Those horses would make a lot of difference to them.

It was plain that Jenkyn had returned here for some particular purpose. He stopped, listening, looking furtively around, then, satisfied, crossed to the foot of a big cottonwood. Scraping away leaves and rubble from the big roots that branched outward in a V, he delved, straightened with an object so heavy that he lifted it with difficulty.

Rawls made out a pair of saddlebags. Jenkyn hoisted them to his shoulder, turned toward one of the horses. The river ran past below a high bank, the water at its base swift and savage, sucking into a whirlpool as it struck the bank and was turned.

Rawls slipped toward the outlaw, moving furtively. Whatever Jenkyn was about, he'd be no more likely to welcome their observation than that of the Indians. He'd proved himself a renegade and turncoat, and Rawls was of no mind to trust him.

He had almost covered the space between when a small stick cracked underfoot. Jenkyn spun about, his blotched face losing color, his eyes darting and wicked. Rawls jumped at him.

Jenkyn was like a cornered animal—and just as dangerous. His hand swept up, clutching a long knife, and he slashed savagely. It was a tricky blow, like the darting of a snake, and almost as hard to avoid. Rawls managed to twist partly to the side, but the blade caught and ripped through his shirt sleeve, slashing from the shoulder down, the edge of the blade coursing like a hot iron, blood spurting in its wake.

Rawls was barely conscious of the pain, for now they were locked together, each fighting for possession of the knife.

The outlaw was unexpectedly wiry, and fighting with the desperation of a man who knows that he must win or die. Twice he almost tore his hand loose with the knife, and twice Rawls managed to thwart him. Then Jenkyn twisted, heaving, and the slippery leaves which were thick underfoot aided him. Rawls lost his footing and went down heavily, Jenkyn uppermost, the knife lifting, ready for a plunge that would end it.

Chapter Twelve

There was nothing that Rawls could do, no chance to turn the blade or evade its sweep. A couple of seconds would give him time enough, but Jenkyn was a true disciple of the Innocents—they who gave the other fellow no chance, but murdered as a matter of policy.

Something moved beneath their struggling bodies, a slippery, slithering form instinctive with horror. It reared a flat ugly head at lightning speed and struck with blind ferocity, and the fangs buried themselves in Jenkyn's descending arm, striking through the shirt sleeve, then caught and clung in the cloth. The outlaw's scream tore his throat, and the deflected knife buried itself in the ground, shearing off the rattles that had commenced belatedly to sound their warning.

There seemed no end to that high bubbling scream. Jenkyn lunged to his feet, running blindly. As Rawls stood up, he was in time to see a stumbling tumble that sent the outlaw over the steep bank and down to the tormented waters.

Kathleen came to him, her eyes big with question. "Did—did it—" she faltered, and could not frame the words with stiffened lips.

Rawls shook his head, his own face drained of color. "Never touched me," he reassured her, and fought down an inclination toward sickness.

For the first time he became aware of the blood on his arm. Kathleen examined the wound, her eyes full of concern.

"It needs binding up," she said. "Wait."

She turned her back, and there was a sound of rending cloth; then she bandaged the gash expertly. Rawls was tempted to loiter, but remembering Jenkyn's scream, he turned to the horses. "We'd better be getting out of here."

Jenkyn had loaded the saddlebags. Not waiting to see what they might contain, they mounted and swung the horses downstream. The Indians were ahead now, but the *Varina* was downriver. With fresh mounts, there was a possibility that, by traveling steadily the rest of the day and through the night, they might overtake the boat.

It would be a grueling ride, tired as they were. Rawls had hoped for a gun, but there was none

on either horse, and Jenkyn had carried his revolver to river bottom. Still, they could not put
up much of a fight with one gun, nor would it
be advisable to shoot game, however hungry they
might be. A shot would be heard far.

Apparently the Indians were well down the
valley, for that last cry from the outlaw brought
no one to investigate. The horses were fresh, the
saddles a relief after riding bareback.

They rode alertly for a while, but relaxed as
the valley remained empty. Kathleen looked hopefully across as she shifted position.

"I don't suppose there's food, by any chance, in
those saddlebags?"

"I doubt it, but we'll have a look," Rawls answered, and pulled to a stop. Kathleen slid stiffly
to the ground, glad of a moment's respite. Rawls
lifted the bags down, startled at their weight.
They were tied tightly, and he fumbled the
knots loose, got them open. Kathleen crowded
close.

Inside were four stout canvas sacks, each one
tied in turn. Even as he lifted the first one out,
feeling the solid chunk it made as he set it down,
Rawls knew what they contained. Gold.

"Looks like he must have made a haul as he was

leaving the gold camps," he said. "He'd cached it there when he came on board the other day, and he didn't want anybody to know about it."

Kathleen stared with quickening breath, but it was not the gold itself that held her attention. On each sack a symbol had been painted, vaguely resembling in design the Masonic insignia. This was a crossed pick and shovel, and inside the inverted V thus formed was the letter G.

"Garrison," Kathleen breathed, and touched a sack with a tentative finger. "That's our mark, Denny! My brother worked it out and sent me a copy almost a year ago!"

She did not voice the unspoken question in both their minds. Here was further proof that this gold had come from Alder or Virginia City, and it had been stolen from the Garrison Company. It was unlikely that Kathleen's father and brother had taken this from the mines. Rather, it represented dealings and profits over a period of months in business. Had murder accompanied theft?

Rawls estimated that there was fifty thousand dollars, mostly in nuggets. Its loss would mean bankruptcy to the firm, aside from the investment made in the *Varina* and its wandering cargo. Thoughtfully he tied the sacks again.

"There must have been some high old times in those camps this last winter," he commented. "The chances are that others of the Innocents were involved in stealing this—likely some of the men who were hanged. Jenkyn got next to where it was cached, and when he pulled out, he took it along. If he'd headed straight out of the country, say for Salt Lake, he might have gotten away. But he figured there was an extra chance for profit by working with the Sioux and looting the boats, for he'd cadged on to that letter Whirter had written. And of course if he sided with the Indians, he figured to be safe in travelin' across their territory."

Rawls divided the gold, placing half behind each saddle.

"It's up to us to get back to the *Varina* with this, and to deliver it to your brother again," he said.

"I wish it was bacon and beans and flour." Kathleen sighed. "I'm so starved—and sore—" She bit off the words and attempted to smile.

"We'll rest and eat pretty soon," Rawls assured her. "We don't want to follow too close on the heels of the Indians during the day, and the horses need to be kept as fresh as possible. But if you can make a few more miles—"

"Lead the way," she agreed. "All I have to do is ride."

He understood the gallantry in that from his own bruises and aches, realizing that she must be suffering even more acutely. But there was no choice. The gold was an added burden that might well prove to be the difference between life and death, but it could not be thrown away.

Anxiously Rawls scanned the far horizon, but there was no further glimpse of smoke down the river. That meant that Earnshaw, having decided to get out of this country, was losing no time. If he had a good day, he'd be safe enough from the Indians. But he'd also be hopelessly out of their reach.

Luck favored them for the next few hours. They were able to keep straight down the valley, not forced to take to the hills or to detour for thick woods or swales, and they encountered no one. Now and again Rawls could see the fresh marks of hoofs where the Sioux were ahead of them, likewise in a race against time.

Near noon, coming to a small stream that joined the river, Rawls pulled up, within the cover of trees.

"You sleep a while," he instructed Kathleen,

as he hobbled the horses and removed the saddles. "I'll get dinner."

"How?" she demanded.

"There was a piece of string in the saddlebags," he said, and showed her. "It will serve as a fishing line, and I have a pin that can be bent for a hook. If I have any luck angling, we'll feast."

"I'm starved, but I'm too sleepy to watch—or help," Kathleen confessed, and curling up beside the saddles, she was instantly asleep.

Rawls was strongly tempted to stretch out for a few minutes of relaxation, but he dared not. He was too tired to keep awake if he let down, and he had to keep watch.

He caught grasshoppers, impaled one on his hook, and dangled it over an inviting pool. The trout were receptive. Likewise they were avidly quick, and the hook not too good. His bait was taken half a dozen times in a row before he succeeded in hooking a speckled beauty and flopping it out on the bank beside him.

Within a few minutes he had four nice ones, and he cleaned them, built a small fire and roasted them. Only when they were ready did he waken Kathleen.

She sat up, bemused with sleep, but the aroma

of the trout revived her. They ate, then rode again.

But as the afternoon waned, there was no sign of the *Varina,* not even a faint smudge of smoke. Earnshaw had had a good day's run. It would be like him to travel a while by night, even though the light was poor. If he did, he'd hopelessly outdistance any pursuit.

If, after keeping on all night, they failed to come up with her by daylight, then overtaking the boat was out of the question. All that would remain would be to go warily and hope eventually to reach civilization again. But if the Indians were thwarted in regard to the packet, they'd turn in a renewed and vengeful search for them, and they were traveling too fast to hide their sign.

More than once they were forced to take to the hills, to make detours. But a couple of times they were able to cut across country where the river made a wide bend, and that was partial compensation. By darkfall the horses were tired, the saddles a torment to raw and aching flesh. Kathleen did not complain. But the drawn look of her face smote him.

Temptation grew to stop and snatch an hour or so of sleep. The horses needed the rest and a chance to graze. They'd require that reserve desperately should they stumble upon Indians. But if Rawls fell asleep, he knew that he was too drugged with weariness for even trail instinct to waken him. He'd sleep the night through, and that would not do.

The cloud cover came down again, screening the stars, and that was good. The *Varina* couldn't run in such darkness. He kept going, aware that Kathleen slept in her saddle. There was a possibility of passing the anchored river packet, but being below it wouldn't matter.

Dawn was long in coming. Hunger merged with a multitude of aches, the horses barely plodding. Rawls strained red and swollen eyes for sign of danger or the boat, and saw neither. He stopped, and they washed vigorously in an icy stream, allowing the horses to crop the grass for half an hour. It was full day by then, and there was a bend in the river half a mile below.

"We'll have a look around that," he promised. "If we don't see it, then we might as well sleep."

He had scant hope of anything save emptiness on the river, but one sign was increasingly ominous—the fact that for nearly twenty-four hours they had encountered none of the Sioux. That absence had a sinister feel.

It was hard to keep alert, even after the water

in their faces. But as they came where the down-sweep of the Yellowstone could be seen again, Rawls jerked wide-awake. It looked as though they were in time—time to be in at the finish.

There was the *Varina,* but she was not moving proudly or disdainfully. The packet was hard aground, apparently on a sand bar, with hardly fifty feet of current separating her from the bank. Those on board were working with a frantic desperation in an attempt to get her off, with scant hope of doing so in time.

For the absence of the Indians was explained. Gathered on the bank, shouting and gesticulating, were full two hundred painted warriors. They had caught up, and were grouped, determined that this time they'd overwhelm and kill.

Kathleen was painfully wide-awake as she viewed the sight. The months of the upriver journey had taught her enough that she could see the apparent hopelessness of the situation.

"And we can't even get to them!" she said protestingly.

Rawls was studying the outlook, his fatigue forgotten. The water between the *Varina* and the near shore was deep—too deep for the Indians to come at the boat from this side. Earn-

shaw had been steering for that deep, clear channel, and probably the tricky light of late evening
or early dawn had fooled him, grounding the
boat before he suspected the hidden bar. Now,
though the paddle wheel churned frantically and
black smoke gushed from the stacks, the *Varina*
did not stir.

The Indians quieted, the chiefs taking counsel
together. Flat open ground stretched back from
the water for a quarter of a mile, and they had
ridden in impressive circles and maneuvers, yelling and shaking bows and tomahawks, or flourish-
ing rifles. But that added up to exactly nothing,
and the leaders had been quick to see it.

Now they had seen what had already occurred
to Rawls, and were starting to put it into execution—a plan which, given just a little time, could
not fail. Kathleen watched, bewildered, as all
the warriors except one started riding downstream, leaving the *Varina* temporarily unboth-
ered.

"Where are they going?" she asked.

"They'll be able to ford the river a mile downstream," Rawls pointed out, indicating riffles
which marked shallow water. He remembered
this section well from the difficulty in getting the
boats past it.

Kathleen's eyes clouded as she understood. So, too, did those on the *Varina*. They had quit the useless effort to get off under their own power, and, knowing that there would be no time for grasshoppering, were preparing to make as good a stand as possible and at least go down fighting.

The cannon was being hastily turned about so that it might be used the other way. Too hastily. The decks of the grounded boat sloped somewhat, and excited men failed to take precautions. The heavy cannon, let loose, started to roll, broke away and plunged through the railing, sank in the deep water at the side. A stunned silence followed.

"Now they haven't a chance!" Kathleen cried.

Certainly there wouldn't be much of a chance of fighting the others off. Once the Sioux crossed the river, they would come back up on the far shore, and though there was a wide stretch of water on that side, it was all so shallow that men either on foot or ahorse could splash straight across to the stranded craft and swarm aboard. A few would be picked off by the riflemen, but the impetus of the charge, the overwhelming weight of numbers, made the result a foregone conclusion.

"Isn't there anything we can do?" Kathleen asked despairingly.

"Yes," Rawls agreed. He'd been watching, calculating closely, wondering if those on board wouldn't see it and make a try. It wouldn't do to move too soon, for some of the stragglers heading downstream might see them and ride back in time to spoil everything. Neither would it do to wait too long, for the *Varina* must be afloat again before the attack could reach her, and it would mean close timing at best.

Earnshaw had seen the chance. A man was preparing to leap overboard, with a coil of light line slung over his shoulder, to swim for the shore. Riflemen were on the deck to give him such protection as they could, but it was a bad business. The warrior crouching behind the big cottonwood, the single tree at the water's edge directly across from the *Varina,* could pick any swimmers off as they came. He was protected by the tree from bullets from the boat.

Now he was fitting an arrow to his bow as the swimmer was in the water. The string drew taut, and Rawls sent his horse surging ahead. Kathleen, not waiting, was at his heels.

The Sioux caught the sound of hoofs, turned. For an instant the bow wavered as he stared in consternation, and that was long enough. Rawls' running horse hit him as he leaped afoot, bowling him back. The warrior spun, strove to check himself, and fell headlong to the water.

Men on deck exclaimed incredulously, recognizing them. Forgetting the imminence of peril, they crowded for a better look. Narcissus' black face appeared, shiny with excited welcome, and she waved wildly.

Rawls dismounted to give the swimmer a hand up the bank, then pulled the rope in, hand over hand. Never had he been so stiff and sore, but he managed a sort of rough skill. Manila cable, used for grasshoppering, was fastened to the lighter cord. He got hold of that, wrapped it about the tree and tied it, and his job was done.

The other end of the cable was already fastened to the capstan, and smoke poured in a fresh cloud from the stacks, the paddle wheel began to revolve again, slowly this time, winding up the rope. It was the same process as grasshoppering, but with the big cottonwood for a stout anchor to tug them loose, there would be no delay.

The last of the Indians were crossing down below, the vanguard riding wildly up the far bank, yelling frenziedly as they began to guess that something had gone wrong. But the nearest had not yet reached the opposite shore when the

Varina moved a bit, hesitated, then slid smoothly out into deep water.

His face a broad smile, Earnshaw twisted the wheel and ran it almost alongside—close enough for Rawls to toss aboard the saddlebags, for Kathleen, the sailor, and himself to leap to the deck. Kathleen stumbled and would have fallen but Narcissus caught and gathered her in welcoming arms.

"My lan', honey, yo' do look a sight, but yo' is sho a sight fo' sore eyes, jus' the same," she crooned. "An' right now I'm puttin' yo' to bed, fo' a good, long, *safe* sleep! The tea come out mighty cleah, this mawnin'—though fo' a while I done thought it mus' be deceivin' me."

"Captain Rawls," Earnshaw said formally, "you are in command. And I never was so happy to see anyone in my life!"

His reasoning had been as Rawls had figured. Seeing the amount of wreckage on the water, there had been no possibility of doubt about the *Astrid* being destroyed. That there would be few if any survivors was a foregone conclusion, and that any of them could escape the Sioux was an even longer chance. His responsibility had been to the living, to the *Varina*. He had acted in the only possible way to insure escape.

Rawls stood by until the *Varina* had passed the portage downriver, while the Indians on shore howled their disappointment. Then, leaving Earnshaw in charge, he slept until the next morning.

The crew, led by Earnshaw, were ready to give their pledge to take no further part in the struggle between the states. That the war would soon be over, none of them doubted. This expedition had been a forlorn hope, but Whirter had inspired them to try. That they had failed was the fortune of war.

"Reckon, if you don't mind, after we get to Benton we'll head for the gold camps and make a fresh start," was the consensus of opinion, and that seemed a fair solution. Only for Astrid there seemed to be none, as she stared at the fleeing shores with stormy eyes.

With the current to aid, the river gradually deepening and widening, the run back to Fort Union was uneventful. Having reported, they proceeded to Fort Benton. That was a hazardous passage, the water low and uncertain. A dozen times they went aground and worked painfully off again. Leaves flamed to a riot of color, then trees and brush were denuded by increasingly bitter winds. Wild geese honked overhead, ice crept out from the shores, the hills turned overnight from brown to white. They came to Benton just ahead of the freeze-up, slush choking the straining paddle wheels. The last boat upriver that season.

There had been a new gold strike at Last Chance, which was said to be even richer than the others, and a new camp had sprung up almost overnight. Every man was intent on his own business, and not much was known of Kathleen's brother, but word was that he had set up anew in Helena, as the new camp was named.

"We'll start the supplies overland by wagon, then ride on ahead and surprise him," Rawls suggested. "Nothing else to do till spring, in any case."

"I think I can sit a saddle again," Kathleen agreed. "But what's the hurry to beat the wagons?"

"Something important." Rawls grinned. "They tell me that the only sky pilot in this section of country should be in Helena for a couple of days, and if we rush, we should catch him there. Your brother can be best man."

"It sounds like a good idea," Kathleen agreed.

"All of it—except for one thing." She drew his face down to hers, her lips quick and tremulous with promise. "He can pretend he is, of course," she whispered, "but for me there's only one best man—or ever can be!"

The End